MW00476797

* * * * * * *

It may have been the mist and drizzle or simply the fact that I had been called here under mysterious circumstances, but the lodge didn't look as inviting as I remembered it. Time and circumstances have a way of making things look different. I'm sure the dismal weather did nothing to brighten up the place, either.

I reached down and turned the key to shut off the engine. It didn't take long after the wipers stopped for the windshield to be so rain splattered that it was impossible to see out.

I sat there for a minute or two as I thought about the sound of Tom's voice on the phone. A cold chill ran through me. I wondered what I was going to find once I went through those large oak doors with their heavy beveled glass windows.

* * * * * * *

Other titles by J.E. Terrall

Western Short Stories
  The Old West
  The Frontier
  Untamed Land

Western Novels
  Conflict in Elkhorn Valley
  Lazy A Ranch
  (A Modern Western)

Romance Novels
  Balboa Rendezvous
  Sing for Me
  Return to Me
  Forever Yours

Mystery/Suspense/Thriller
  I Can See Clearly
  The Return Home
  The Inheritance

Nick McCord Mysteries
  Vol – 1 Murder at Gill's Point
  Vol – 2 Death of a Flower
  Vol – 3 A Dead Man's Treasure
  Vol – 4 Blackjack, A Game to Die For
  Vol – 5 Death on the Lakes

Peter Blackstone Mysteries
  Murder in the Foothills
  Murder on the Crystal Blue
  Murder of My Love

Frank Tidsdale Mysteries
  Death by Design

MURDER AT GILL'S POINT
VOL 1

A Nick McCord Mystery

by
J. E. Terrall

All rights reserved
Copyright © 1996 by J. E. Terrall
Revised 2008

ISBN: 978-0-9844591-7-9

No part of this book may be reproduced or transmitted in any form or by any means, electronic or mechanical, including photocopying, recording or by any information storage or retrieval system, in whole or in part, without the expressed written consent of the author.

This is a work of fiction. Names, characters, and incidents are either a product of the author's imagination or are used fictitiously, and any resemblance to actual persons, living or dead, is purely coincidental.

Printed in the United States of America
First & Second Printing / 2008 – www.lulu.com
Third Printing   / 2013 – www.createspace.com

Cover: Front cover designed by Phyllis Terrall
          Photographed by J.E. Terrall

Book Layout/
Formatting: J.E. Terrall
              Custer, South Dakota

MURDER AT GILL'S POINT
VOL 1

A Nick McCord Mystery

To my wife for all her continued help and
encouragement as I continue to write.

CHAPTER ONE

I'd been working rather late in an effort to wrap up a case that had been particularly difficult. I was anxious to get home and kick back to relax for a little while. Maybe even spend a little time in front of the television watching something that I didn't have to think about.

Normally I like to fix my own dinner, but I was tired and didn't want the hassle. There was a KFC near my apartment so I stopped in on the way home and grabbed a three-piece chicken dinner from the Colonel.

Climbing the stairs to my small third floor apartment, I was really looking forward to some time to myself. Just as I turned to start up the last set of stairs, I could hear my phone ringing so I hurried on up the stairs in the hope of catching it before whoever was calling hung up.

When I reached the landing at the top of the stairs, I was already fumbling for my keys. Finding the key to my apartment, I shoved it into the lock and unlocked the door as quickly as possible. I entered my apartment and hurried across the room toward the phone, dropping my dinner on the coffee table as I reached out and picked up the receiver. I was almost certain there would be no one on the other end by now.

"Hello?" I said half expecting to get nothing but a dial tone.

"Nick, is that you?"

It was a man's voice on the other end of the line and it had the inescapable sound of relief that he had finally gotten hold of me. I also noted a hint of panic in his question. Although the voice sounded a bit familiar, I couldn't immediately place it.

"Yes. Who's this?"

"It's Tom, Tom Walker."

"Tom! What's up?"

It had been a long time since I had heard from him.

"Nick, I have a very big favor to ask of you," he said, getting right to the point.

My excitement in hearing from him sort of slipped away. I couldn't put my finger on it, but there was something strange about the sound of his voice. It seemed a little shaky as if he were frightened of something or someone.

"Sure," I said as my concerns for my old friend began to fill my thoughts. "What is it? Are you in some sort of trouble?"

"No," he replied quickly, almost too quickly for me to believe him.

"Then what is it?"

"I know this is going to sound rather strange, but I need you to come up to the lodge as soon as you can. I really need to talk to you. It's very important."

I could hear the urgency in his voice.

"Sure. I can be up there in a couple of days, if that's okay?" I replied knowing that it might be hard to clear my schedule and get my boss to let me go on such short notice.

"Great. That'll be great. I'll be waiting," he said sounding relieved.

The change in his voice when I said I would come was like that of a frightened child who called home from summer camp because he was homesick and heard a familiar voice reassuring him everything was all right. However, Tom was no frightened child. He was obviously very nervous about something, but what? Based on past experience with Tom, it was not like him to be frightened of anything. I had always considered him to be the most levelheaded person I know.

"Tom, what's wrong?"

"I can't talk now, Nick. I'll explain everything when you get here," then the phone suddenly went dead.

As I set the receiver down in the cradle, I began to think about Tom. Tom Walker and I go back a long way. We attended the University of Wisconsin in Madison together. He studied business while I was interested in criminology. We enjoyed the same sports, the same kinds of music and on one occasion we even chased the same woman.

We became good friends during those years in college. As time went by, our friendship continued to grow even though we went our own separate ways and lived miles apart. We often went for several years without seeing each other, but every time we got together it was as if we had seen each other just a day or so ago.

As I sat down on the sofa and opened my chicken dinner, my mind went back to the last time I had seen him. It was several years ago. Tom had purchased a very large old house near Gill's Rock, Wisconsin. He was like a kid with a new toy. Running a lodge on the shore of the Lake Michigan had been a long time dream of his.

At his insistence, I drove all the way up to Gill's Rock to help him celebrate the closing of the deal. He was excited about the challenge of taking the huge old house and turning it into a year-round vacation lodge. The old place was located on the shore of Lake Michigan, near the tip of a peninsula.

As I started to eat my dinner, my thoughts quickly returned to Tom's call. I hadn't really planned to take a vacation just yet; but when an old friend calls and says that he needs to see me as soon as possible, I couldn't very well refuse his request.

I found myself thinking about Tom and what he had said. It was the sound of his voice that plagued my mind throughout the remainder of the evening. It was hard for me to put my finger on it, but he sounded as if he had been up all night and was very tired. Although he had tried to sound calm and relaxed, there was an underlying critical need to see me in the tone of his voice, which did not set well with me.

I got very little sleep as I spent a good part of the night trying to figure out what it could be that he would not tell me over the phone. I got the feeling that whatever it was he was afraid that someone might overhear him talking to me. That particular thought caused me to really worry.

Tom had sounded desperate, almost as if it was extremely important that I come as soon as possible. I had a hard time getting over the fact that this was totally out of character for him.

The next morning I went into the Precinct to visit with my captain. I explained my situation and he agreed to let me have a few days off since I had nothing that couldn't wait for a couple of days, and since I had just finished up a rather complicated and very distressing case.

The sound of Tom's voice continued to haunt me throughout the day as I cleared my calendar and finished up a couple of reports. When I arrived home in the evening, I packed my bags and got ready to leave. Once again I didn't get a very good night's sleep.

The following morning, I threw my luggage in the trunk of my car and headed north on Interstate forty-three out of Milwaukee toward Green Bay. I got an early start, well before the morning rush hour traffic. It was overcast and a little chilly for this time of year. The promise of rain hung heavy in the air. I sure hoped that the weather was not some kind of an omen of what I would find once I arrived at Tom's Gill's Point Lodge.

As my old Dodge purred along the highway, my thoughts kept taking me back to Tom and his phone call. Tom had had every advantage that anyone could ask for. He was well liked, had a good education, a friendly personality and he had money. As far as I knew he had a successful business running his lodge. I had to wonder what could possibly have gone wrong.

I was less than an hour out of Milwaukee when it began to rain. It started out slowly, but before long it was coming down in sheets. The worn out wiper blades that I had put off replacing were having a difficult time keeping my windshield clear enough for me to see the road. The going was slow.

By the time I got to Manitowoc, the rain had slowed down and had turned into a steady drizzle. With a little more than an hour or so to go, I left the interstate and followed state highway forty-two all the way to Gill's Rock.

The small town of Gill's Rock was located near the end of a peninsula that sticks out into Lake Michigan and forms one side of Green Bay. I became so interested in the small community that I almost missed the turn off to Gill's Point where Tom's lodge was located.

The weather was still cold and dismal when I pulled up in front of the lodge. Several cars were parked out in front. One was a little red sports car parked near the gate of the white picket fence. The little sports car seemed out of place as the other four cars were large luxury cars like those found in the parking lot of an exclusive country club.

My first impression was that Tom must be doing very well to have guests who drove cars like the ones parked out in front. My beat up old Dodge just didn't seem to fit in very well with the rest of them.

I pulled into a space next to the little red sports car and parked. Before shutting off the ignition, I sat and looked up at the house. My wipers were slowly moving back and forth across my windshield.

As I sat staring at the large old house through my rain splattered windshield, I couldn't help but wonder what this place must have been like when it was first built over a hundred years ago. Tom had bought it when it was pretty run down. If I remembered right, Tom had told me that at one time it had been the summer home of some very rich man, a ship's captain, I believe.

Out in front of the lodge on the lawn was a neatly painted sign that read, "Gill's Point Lodge. Welcome". Behind the sign stood the lodge. It was three stories tall with high peaks and a steeply pitched roof. The lodge was painted a deep dark red. The lacy type of woodwork that trimmed the high pointed gables was painted white. The white trim gave the lodge the appearance of once having been a great mansion.

On both ends of the lodge were tall round towers, each reaching above the roof of the lodge itself and each having a tall slender pointed roof. On the top of the towers were lightning rods that seemed to disappear into the dark, gloomy clouds overhead making it a rather ominous looking building.

The towers on each end of the lodge were four stories high, one story higher than the rest of the house. They had windows at each level. The thought crossed my mind that on a clear day a person should be able to see way out into Lake Michigan from the upper windows in the towers. The unobstructed view from the top floor of the tower would be fantastic. It might even be possible to see over to the other side of the peninsula and out into Green Bay. I was sure that on a clear day, it would be possible to see the ships going in and out of Green Bay, which was undoubtedly the reason that the towers had been built so high.

As I leaned over the steering wheel and looked up toward the top of one of the towers, I thought I saw some movement at one of the windows. I wasn't sure so I leaned closer to the windshield and strained to get a better look, but I could not make out anything. It may have been the reflection of something off the glass, or it may have just been my imagination. Whatever I thought I saw, I could not see it now.

Across the front of the lodge was a long covered porch with very delicate wooden trim and a fancy wooden railing. The skirt around the base of the porch was also done in the same delicate design as the rest of the trim. Even the steps reflected the care that had been taken in designing the house.

I had to admire the care that Tom had taken to maintain the original beauty and workmanship. Tom had done a very nice job of converting the large old house into a lakeside lodge.

It may have been the mist and drizzle or simply the fact that I had been called here under mysterious circumstances, but the lodge didn't look as inviting as I remembered it. Time and circumstances have a way of making things look different. I'm sure the dismal weather did nothing to brighten up the place, either.

I reached down and turned the key to shut off the engine. It didn't take long after the wipers stopped for the windshield to be so rain splattered that it was impossible to see out.

I sat there for a minute or two as I thought about the sound of Tom's voice on the phone. A cold chill ran through me. I wondered what I was going to find once I went through those large oak doors with their heavy beveled glass windows.

As it was still raining, I quickly realized that there was no way for me to keep from getting wet unless I wanted to stay in the car until the rain stopped. Staying in the car didn't seem to me like a very good idea, I could end up being in the car all night. I pulled my coat collar up around my neck and then pushed the car door open. As quickly as possible, I ran up onto the large porch. Once I was in the shelter of the porch roof, I stopped to shake the water off my coat and turn my collar back down before going inside.

"Well, hello, there."

I slowly turned my head to see where that seductive, sexy voice had come from. Sitting under a light on a swing near the end of the porch I discovered a woman, but not just any woman.

The woman appeared to be in her mid-to-late twenties with long flowing blond hair that cascaded softly down onto her shoulders. Her soft blond hair framed a face that was beautiful enough to be on the front cover of any respectable woman's magazine. Her complexion was smooth and her nose had a perfect shape. Her red lips curled up slightly at the corners in a very pleasant smile. Her lips appeared to be soft and warm, to say nothing about inviting. But it was her eyes that really captured my attention. Even in the late afternoon light on a gloomy day they were the most beautiful cobalt blue that anyone could ever hope to see, and they were looking at me over the top of a steaming hot mug of coffee, which she held firmly in both hands.

This extraordinary looking woman was wearing what looked like a warm knitted sweater to keep the chill off. The sweater did little to hide the fact that she had an attractive figure. She was also wearing those tight fitting slacks, the kind with the little stirrups on them, and she had her legs curled up under her.

"Hello," I finally replied.

"Are you one of the guests?" she asked politely.

"Yes. Yes, I am."

The thought raced through my mind that this was a woman who could make my stay here much more pleasant than I had figured on. I would have liked to sit down with her and continue this conversation, but I really needed to find Tom. I didn't want to say too much to anyone until I knew why Tom had asked me to come here.

"I would like to stay and chit-chat with you, but I think I should probably get checked in," I said as I smiled at her.

"Maybe later then," she said with a soft pleasing voice and a beautiful smile.

"Maybe later," I replied.

I found it intriguing that even the dismal weather could not distract from the woman's good looks and pleasant sounding voice. I gave her a brief nod and a smile then turned back toward the door. I reached for the doorknob and turned it. I glanced at the woman one last time before I swung open the door and stepped inside the lodge.

I suddenly found myself in a very large room that seemed to instantly take me back in time at least a hundred years. This was my first opportunity to get a good look at the inside of the lodge since Tom bought and restored it. I stood there in the entryway as I looked around taking in the massiveness of the room as well as the charm of the old house.

The main room was exceptionally large and had several clusters of chairs and sofas arranged neatly into small conversational groupings. The ceiling was very high and had large open beams that crisscrossed the white stucco ceiling.

The large open staircase was made of polished walnut and the railing had been painstakingly restored. Each rung in the banister had been carefully hand finished. It struck me as more of a work of art then as a functional staircase.

The long wall opposite the staircase was paneled in a rich, polished walnut with lots of bookshelves filled with old books that gave a certain dignity to the room, as well as a touch of color. In the center of the wall there was a large gray stone fireplace that looked as if it were big enough that a six foot long log could be burned in it without cutting it up. The massive fire screen in front of the fireplace reminded me of the delicate ironwork of a garden gate much like the ones that might be found in the French Quarter of New Orleans. The detail and the workmanship of the work were excellent.

Above the fireplace was an old life-size oil painting of a man. The painting was in a large gold frame typical of those used by the very wealthy in the eighteen hundreds. The man in the painting had a full red beard with just a touch of gray mixed in it, a full head of hair with some graying at the temples and eyes of steel gray. Looking very carefully at the painting, it gave me an eerie feeling that he was looking back at me. I got the impression that no matter where a person might stand in the room, the man in the picture would be looking directly at them.

From the type of clothes the man in the painting was wearing, I would have bet a weeks pay that he was a ship's captain, probably the captain on one of the larger sailing ships that roamed the Great Lakes in the mid-to-late eighteen hundreds. The expression on his face was that of a man who was very serious about everything. He did not look like the type of man who could be trifled with, unless of course, you wanted to feel his wrath.

"Nick!"

I immediately recognized the excited voice behind me, but I was so captivated by the picture that I didn't bother to turn around and offer a greeting. Instead I simply asked, "Tom, who's that man?"

"That is none other than the infamous Captain Bartholomew Samuelson. He was the one who had this house built."

"From the looks of him, I don't think I would like to be crew member on one of his ships."

"Me, either," Tom agreed.

"How are you, Tom?" I said as I turned around and offered him my hand.

I froze in my tracks as I looked at my old friend. I was shocked when I saw how much Tom had changed over the past few years. Forgetting the fact that we were both a few years older since we had seen each other, I found it hard to believe how much he had changed.

Tom stood with a slight slouch of his shoulders that was more typical of a tired old man. He looked as if he had been in very poor health for sometime. The dark circles under his eyes, the tired look on his face and the considerable gray in his hair gave me reason for concern. It took me a second or two to get over the shock of seeing him like that.

"I'm glad you could come," he said softly as he shook my hand.

"I couldn't refuse an invitation from an old friend," I said.

I was immediately sorry that I had used the term "old" under the circumstances. He appeared to be at least ten or fifteen years older then me, when in fact I was actually three months older then Tom. Even his grip of my hand didn't have the firmness that I remembered.

"Please, come with me," he said as he took hold of my arm and led me toward the large open staircase.

I hadn't missed the fact that Tom seemed to be acting very strange, speaking softly and quickly glancing about the room every few seconds. It was almost as if he were afraid that someone might see us together, or possibly hear what we were saying. He seemed to be in a hurry to get me someplace where we could talk privately, away from any of the guests.

As I followed Tom up the stairs, I glanced back over my shoulder into the main room. I noticed an old man in the corner. I hadn't seen him earlier, but he was sitting in a large wingback chair in the far corner of the room. He was wearing a dark suit and holding a newspaper as if he was reading it.

Even though he was clear across the room, I could feel him watching me. He looked harmless enough, but there was something about him that gave me the willies. For one thing, he never took his eyes off me as I followed Tom up the stairs. I found it interesting that he didn't even seem to care that I saw him watching me. Anytime someone watches me that closely, I tend to get nervous and want to know why.

CHAPTER TWO

When Tom and I reached the top of the stairs, I followed him down the long hall. I put aside my concerns about the old man I had seen downstairs and looked down the second floor hall.

The carpet in the hall was a dark red and very soft under my feet. I made note of the fact that one could easily move up and down the hall without making a sound. The walls were covered with red and gold flocked wallpaper. There were old gaslights that had been converted to electric lights next to the door of each room.

I noticed there were a number of nicely framed photos on the walls in the hall. The photos were in old fashion frames to help keep the time period and style of the lodge throughout. All the photos looked as if they were of family members, but of whose family I had no idea.

As we walked along the hall, my attention returned to Tom. I noticed that Tom seemed to walk slower then I remembered, and the spring in his step was gone. He stopped at the third door on the left, took a key out of his pocket and unlocked the door. I glanced at the number on the door. It was room number five. I wondered how many rooms Tom had that he rented in the lodge. After opening the door, he handed me the key as he held the door for me.

"This is your room," he said as he waited for me to go inside.

I stepped past Tom and entered the room. He followed me into the room and quickly closed the door behind us. I didn't bother to look the room over because Tom's general appearance continued to plague me. There was something terribly wrong and I wanted to know what it was more than I cared about the room. Tom had always been an athletic person, strong and healthy, but now he looked weak and frail. I wondered what could have caused such a drastic change in him in so few years. Maybe he had been sick or he was ill with cancer. Whatever it was, I had to know. I needed to know so that I could hopefully help him in some way.

As I turned around to face him, I said, "Tom, we've known each other far too long for me to beat around the bush. So I'm going to come out with it. What is going on around here? You look like hell."

I was suddenly saddened by the look in Tom's eyes as he bowed his head and looked down at the floor. It almost made me wish I had not been so blunt in my comments.

He slowly walked across the room toward a chair. It was easy to see that he knew he had changed.

As I watched him, it became clear to me that he was trying to put his thoughts together. He dropped down in the chair as if he were totally exhausted and then looked up at me. It was a moment or two before he spoke.

"Nick, I don't know what's going on."

The tone of his voice reflected his frustration and his inability to understand what was happening here.

"Why don't you try filling me in on what you do know? Have you been sick?"

"No, not really," he said with a sigh before he continued. "Nick, I haven't gotten a good night's sleep for the past three, almost four months."

Tom leaned forward putting his elbows on his knees and his face in his hands. There was no doubt in my mind there was something very wrong. I don't think I could describe just how I was feeling at that moment. One of my longtime friends had been put through so much stress, or something, that it turned him into a frail, tired old man long before his time.

"Tell me. What's been going on that has kept you from getting sleep?"

"I don't know," he sighed.

"Then tell me what you do know," I suggested, hoping he would say something that would allow me to help him.

"It's a long story, Nick," he said as he looked up at me with sad, tired eyes.

"I have a longtime to listen. That's why I came up here," I reminded him as I pulled up a chair and sat down in front of him.

I watched Tom as he sat quietly trying to gather his thoughts. I could see in his eyes that what was bothering him was not likely to be the normal problems that come with owning a business like his. Whatever it was that had gotten him to this state was going to take sometime for him to explain. I would have to be patient with him. He sat there for several minutes before looking up again to speak.

"It all started this past winter, about three or four months ago. The winter had been unusually cold and the lake was full of large jagged chunks of ice.

"One very cold early morning I went for a walk along the beach like I do every morning. Well, like I used to do before all this happened," he added softly.

"While I was out for my walk, I discovered a large chunk of ice that had been pushed up on the beach by the changing currents near the point. The block of ice was different from any I had seen in the past."

"How was it different?" I asked as much to keep him talking as to get information.

"It was about three foot square and a little over six foot long. A block of ice that size being pushed up on the beach is not all that unusual around here, especially during a hard cold winter like we had this year," he explained.

"We often get large pieces of ice pushed up on the beach, but this one was unusual in two ways. First of all it was fairly smooth, almost as if it had been cut out of a larger piece of ice. It wasn't the usual jagged odd shaped pieces of ice that usually get pushed up on shore.

"The second unusual thing about the block of ice was the fact that there was a woman frozen inside it."

"A woman!"

It would have been a gross understatement to say that what he said piqued my interest. It isn't everyday that a person finds a woman frozen in a block of ice lying on the beach in front of the house. That just doesn't happen.

"That's right, a woman," he said as he looked at the expression on my face. "But it was not just any woman."

"What do you mean by that, Tom?" I asked as I wondered what other surprises he had in store for me.

"The woman in the ice was the spitting image of Captain Samuelson's young wife, Elizabeth Samuelson. She was even wearing the same dress as the one she is wearing in that picture," he said as he pointed to a picture on the wall behind me.

I found what he was saying very hard to believe, but I turned around and looked at the picture Tom had pointed at. The young woman in the picture was a very nice looking young woman. She had long dark hair, which cascaded down over her shoulders in long ringlets and curls. Her eyes were dark and there was a smile on her face that would indicate she was very happy, at least when the picture was taken.

I noticed that the woman in the picture was wearing a long white dress typical of dresses worn around the turn of the century. She was sitting on the front porch of this very house.

On closer examination of the photo, I discovered that she was not only an exceptionally beautiful woman, but the dress she was wearing was a summer dress. It was not the type of dress one would expect to see worn during the winter months. A closer look at her surroundings indicated that the picture had been taken in the summer. There were flowers in the flowerbed near the porch and the trees had leaves on them.

"Did you call the police?" I asked as I turned back to look at him.

"Yes, of course."

"I take it the police were out here to investigate?"

"Sure. They were all over the place for three or four days. They spent weeks trying to figure out who the woman was. I tried to tell them who she was, but they didn't seem to want to believe me," he said, his voice showing his disappointment.

"I don't think you could blame them for that. Did they come up with any answers at all?" I asked.

"Not a clue," Tom said with a hint of frustration in his voice. "They never were able to make a positive identification of the woman. They had all kinds of theories, made all kinds of speculations about how she got in the block of ice in the first place, but in the end they all came up empty.

"I still personally believe that the body in the block of ice was that of Elizabeth Samuelson, Captain Samuelson's wife," he said, for the first time his voice sounding like he knew what he was talking about.

"What makes you so sure it was this Elizabeth woman?"

"Who else could it be?" he asked as if there were no other possibilities.

"Well, it could be almost anyone. For example, a distant relative, someone who happens to look a lot like her, who knows?"

"But it wasn't just anyone. I know it was her," Tom insisted.

It was difficult for me to see Tom like this. No matter how impossible it was for me to believe him, Tom certainly believed in what he was saying. Tom had always been a very rational man, not easily taken in by some bizarre happening, or some wild scheme. It was not like him to go off on some wild tangent, either. I had to do something to get him back to reality.

"Do you have any idea when Elizabeth died?" I asked.

"No, but according to what little I have been able to find out about her, she disappeared sometime in May or June of eighteen ninety-eight. She would have been twenty-four or possibly twenty-five years old," he said as a matter of fact.

"Come on, Tom, that's over a hundred years ago. If she had been dead that long, there would be nothing left of her except for possibly a few bones and even that's not likely."

"I knew you wouldn't believe me if I explained all this to you on the phone. That's why I had to have you come up here."

The look in Tom's eyes was that of a very desperate man. I could see that he was convinced the woman was who he thought she was, but how could that be?

"Tom, if the body was really that of Elizabeth, - ah, - what's-her-name."

"Samuelson, Elizabeth Samuelson."

"Okay, Samuelson. If the woman in the block of ice was really the woman you think it was, she would have decomposed a long time ago," I said in an effort to get Tom to hear what he was telling me.

"But she was frozen in ice," he insisted.

"Tell me, how could she possibly have been frozen in ice for all those years and still be in the lake? The lake continually thaws and freezes each year. It's impossible," I said.

"I know," he said with a note of frustration in his voice. "That's what doesn't make any sense."

"It sure doesn't," I had to agree.

"That's not all," Tom added.

By now I was ready for almost anything Tom might have to say. I thought I had heard everything, but I was soon to find out that I had just heard the beginning.

"Ever since Elizabeth's body showed up on my beach, I have hardly gotten any sleep. I hear strange noises in the middle of the night and see strange movements in the halls," he said as he looked at me and wondered if there was any way that I could possibly believe him.

"Tom, I want you to take your time and think clearly. Just what is it you think you saw?"

"I did see it," he said defensively.

"Okay. Okay. What did you see?"

"I - - I saw a young woman, or what looked like a young woman sort of float across the main room of the lodge and again in the hall."

"Was it Elizabeth you saw?"

"I don't know, but it could have been. I couldn't make out her face very well," Tom replied, not to sure himself.

"When did you see her?"

"I saw her twice. The first time was two weeks after I found Elizabeth's body on the beach. She sort of floated across the main room."

"When was the second time?"

"I saw her again several nights after that, only that time it was in the hallway on the second floor."

I took a minute to think about what he was saying. I had been to Disneyland and had seen how they made ghosts appear and how they made them move. What he was telling me was a little easier for me to understand, but why would someone go to all that trouble?

"Were both times at night?" I asked as I thought about what he was telling me.

"Yes. Is that important?" he asked as he looked to me for information.

"I don't know, but it could be. Tell me about the noises that you heard?"

"Shortly after the last time I saw - ah, - - the ghost, I started hearing strange noises. It sounded like old squeaky doors opening and closing, and a little like the wind whistling through tree branches or telephone wires. Something like that."

"Could the squeaking doors have been guests opening and closing doors to their rooms?"

"No. I thought of that. I checked all the doors. None of them squeaked."

"Okay. It was just a thought. Go on," I suggested.

"On a few occasions I heard voices, but I could never make out what was being said. It was always just mumbling, you know, like voices coming through a tunnel or something."

"Has anyone else seen the ghost, or heard any of these strange noises or complained about strange noises?"

"No," he said softly. "I have not had one single complaint about anything from any of my guests. I have even asked a few guests if they heard any strange sounds during the night, and they all have said that they didn't hear anything. I seem to be the only one hearing the voices."

I took a minute to stop and think. Everything had an explanation. That much I knew. There was a reason for the noises, and a reason that he was the only one hearing them.

"Obviously, you called me up here because you trust me and know that you can tell me anything. If you told anyone else what you have told me, they'd have you locked away by now. Just what is it you want me to try to do for you?"

"Nick, you're my best friend. I trust you more than anyone. Back in college, you were always able to solve every mystery story you ever read before anyone else. You always seemed to be able to figure out what happened and why long before anyone else. I want you to help me find out what is going on here before I go completely crazy. Hell, I'm probably already there. I'm just too crazy to know it," he said with a note of despair in his voice.

I didn't know what to think. It took me a few minutes to try to put together what he had told me. If someone was trying to drive my friend crazy, they certainly had a very good start. But why? What possible reason could anyone have for doing this to him?

"Okay, Tom, I will try to find out what is going on here. But first I want to know if there is someone around here that dislikes you? Do you have any enemies, or maybe someone you just plain pissed off?"

Tom gave my question some thought before replying to it. "No. No one I know of."

"Think. Maybe you had a customer that didn't like the service he got, or didn't like the food? Maybe someone that you have had an argument with in the past, say, six or seven months, or even in the past year?"

"I have not had a single guest that wasn't perfectly satisfied with the service or the meals."

"Are you sure? It seems to me that something would upset a guest sooner or later."

"I have not received a single complaint. If someone was not happy with my food, his room, or the service he got here, he didn't say anything to me or my staff about it," he said with a slight hint of pride.

"Do you get along with everyone in town?"

"Yes, of course," he replied.

"What about your neighbors?"

"No problems there. I don't have any close neighbors. The closest one is maybe three-quarters of a mile down the road."

"Is your property of any real great value to someone else, other than its value as a lodge?"

"Not that I know of."

"Has anyone shown an interest in buying this place, say, in the past year or so?"

"No. Wait a minute," he said as his eyes lit up as he remembered something. "There was an elderly gentleman who came to the lodge about four, maybe five months ago that wanted to know if I would be interested in selling the lodge. But when I told him I wasn't interested in selling, he left. I never saw or heard from him again."

"How did he react when you told him it was not for sale? Did he seem upset or angry?" I asked.

"No, not at all. He was very pleasant and thanked me. Like I said, I never saw or heard from him again."

"After the body was found on the beach, did your business drop off?"

"No, as a matter of fact it improved for a little while."

"Is business still up?"

"Well, no, not really. It's down just a little for this time of year. I think I have two empty rooms if I count your room. I'm usually full this time of year," he admitted.

"Nick, you do believe me, don't you?"

"Sure," I replied, but there was a certain doubt in my mind.

Tom seemed very much relieved when I reassured him that I believed him. He even appeared to look a little better, but that may have been because he had someone he could talk to about what was happening to him.

"I have to leave for now," Tom said as he stood up. "I have to make sure that dinner is on the table and on time for our guests. We eat at six o'clock sharp."

"Okay. I'll see you at dinner."

I watched Tom as he walked across the room toward the door. As he reached for the doorknob, he stopped and looked back at me.

"Thanks, Nick," he said softly. "Thanks for coming."

I could see in his eyes that he was very grateful I had come. I watched him as he turned and left the room. I didn't know what I could do for him, but I had to try. I was convinced that if something wasn't done soon, there was no telling what might happen to him. He might even go over the edge and end up in a mental hospital. I couldn't let that happen.

I spent the next few minutes mulling over in my head everything Tom had told me. It all sounded so bizarre, but I had never known Tom to lie. Nothing seemed to make any sense, at least from what Tom was able to tell me. Past experience had told me that there is a logical reason for everything. All I had to do was find it.

As I looked around the room, I realized that I needed to get a feel for the lodge and its history. From what I could see on the walls, I figured that there was no better place to start than right here in my room.

The furnishings in the room were typical of those straight out of the late eighteen hundreds. The dresser stood on short delicately carved legs and had an oval beveled edged glass mirror on the top. The bed was a large four-poster bed with a ruffled white linen canopy. The small desk was on long delicately carved legs of the same design as the dresser and it had several small pigeonholes that held paper, envelopes and such on the top.

The walls of the room were covered with gold wallpaper that had a red flocked design on it. The lights had the appearance of gaslights typical of those in the late eighteen hundreds, but they had been converted to electric.

The room looked fantastic. Although the outside of the lodge had appeared to look a little dreary, probably due to the weather, the inside was bright, cheery and comfortable, and decorated perfectly.

I had gotten so wrapped up in the decor of the room that I almost overlooked the pictures on the walls. Even the pictures reflected the era. The first picture I examined was the one of Elizabeth Samuelson that Tom had pointed out earlier. I was sure the photo was a touched up copy of the original, but it was a very good one. It looked like it may have lost some of the characteristics of photos of its day when it was copied, but it was still quite clear. It would be difficult to prove whether it really was Mrs. Samuelson, or someone who looked very much like her without the original photo. I would have liked to have had the original photo to examine.

There were several other photos on the wall, but none as interesting as the one of the woman. I still examined each photo carefully for some kind of a clue. A clue to what I didn't have the vaguest idea. I still wasn't sure what I was looking for, or if I would even know it if I found it.

After I finished examining the room, I decided that I would go get my things from the car and try to get a little settled in before dinner. As I went downstairs, I looked toward the other side of the room to see if the old man was still sitting in the corner. The chair was empty. I briefly wondered where he might have gone, but it did not seem to be that important at the moment. I would probably find out who he was at dinner.

It was still raining a little as I took my luggage out of the trunk. As I started back into the lodge, I glanced toward the porch swing to see if the woman was still there. When I saw she was no longer on the porch, I figured that it had gotten too cool outside and she must have gone in.

When I returned to my room and was putting the key in the door, I had the strangest feeling that I was being watched. I quickly turned around, but the only thing I saw was a door down the hall slowly close and the muffled sound of the latch catching. It was the second time I had gotten the feeling that someone was taking just a little too much interest in my being there.

Once in my room, I locked the door. I went to the bathroom and washed my face. It was too early for dinner, so I laid down on the bed. I didn't plan to sleep, just to lie there and think about what Tom had told me and what I had already observed.

There were a lot of questions to be answered, and I had no idea where to begin. At best it was a long shot, but maybe one of the guests would provide me with a starting point. I would have to wait and see. Until I had a chance to meet the other guests, I figured that I might as well lay back and let my mind wonder over what little I did know.

CHAPTER THREE

As I lay on the bed with my hands behind my head looking up at the ceiling, my thoughts were of Tom and his problem, which had suddenly become my problem. I was having a hard time trying to put together everything that he had told me in an effort to make some sense out of it. I wasn't sure just what to believe, but I knew that Tom was not the sort of man to make things up just for the hell of it, nor was he the type to blow things out of proportion. I guess I would have to say it was the look in Tom's eyes that made me want to believe him.

What he had told me was bizarre as well as interesting, to say the least. But it was also a rather challenging puzzle that I found myself wanting to solve.

It briefly crossed my mind that the whole thing might be some sort of a joke, but that didn't set well with me. Although I had not seen Tom in several years, I had never known him to be a jokester. In fact, he was one of the most serious people I knew. I also felt it would be very difficult for him to look as rundown and tired as he did without something being very wrong.

I also thought that it might be some sort of a joke being played on Tom, but I didn't find it very funny. There was something about what Tom had told me that made me feel it was no joke. I couldn't help but think that there was something of a more sinister nature happening here.

The room Tom had given me for my stay at the lodge was a very quiet room. In fact it was so quiet that I was able to hear the door to the room next to mine open and then close. I normally don't make it a practice of eavesdropping on other people's conversations, but I could hear the sound of voices in the room next to mine.

There was only the sound of one voice coming from the next room that I could really understand any of what was being said. It was a deep, heavy voice, very much typical of a man's voice. The other voice was just sounds that didn't make any sense to me, but were slightly higher pitched. Based on that, I guessed it was the voice of a woman.

"I don't know who he is or what he's doing here," the male voice said. "But then this is a lodge, and guests do come here."

There was a brief bit of mumbling from the voice that was much softer. I couldn't understand what was being said until I heard the heavier voice again.

"I'm not sure, but I don't think he's here to meet with the young woman. I get the impression that he might be a friend of Walker's. If he is, he could turn out to be a problem," the deeper voice said.

There was some more mumbling I could not understand, but at this point I was longer not trying to listen in on the conversation. After all, it was clear that they were talking about me. I have a tendency to like to hear what people have to say about me, especially when they don't know that I'm listening.

"I agree," I heard the male voice say. "We'll have to be more careful with him around, at least until we find out more about him and what he's doing here."

Once again I heard the softer voice say something, but no matter how hard I tried I still couldn't understand it. It was followed by the sound of the room door opening then closing.

I quickly scrambled off the bed and hurried to the door. Being as quiet as I could, I opened the door a crack in the hope of seeing who had just left the room next to mine. I peeked out, but I could not see anyone in the hall. However,

I did hear a door down the hall close. I couldn't see which door it was, or who had been in the next room.

I closed my door as quietly as I could and walked back to the bed. It was suddenly very clear that something was going on here, but I had no idea what it was or who was involved. I was beginning to think that maybe Tom had a very good reason to be worried.

As I stood next to the bed staring at the wall, I began to wonder who was in the room next to mine. There was no doubt in my mind that it would be easy to find out who occupied the room next to mine. All I had to do was ask Tom. However, it might not be so easy to find out who had been visiting that room since I had not seen which room they went into after they left.

The harder question for me to answer was why was I of so much interest to the two people who had just been in the room next door? My next question was; were there only two people in the room, or were there more? I had heard only two different voices, but that didn't leave out the possibility of others in the room.

I sat down on the edge of the bed and stared at the picture of Elizabeth Samuelson. The longer I looked at her, the more fascinated I became with her. It seemed as if she was drawing me toward her, into what had once been her life. There was no doubt in my mind that I wanted to know more about her. I'm not one who believes in ghosts, but I had a feeling I was going to get to know Elizabeth very well before this was over.

That thought made me think of Tom and the fact that he had used the word "ghost" when telling me about what had happened here. Although Tom never actually said she was the ghost, I got the impression he thought that the ghost he had seen might have been the ghost of Elizabeth.

It also occurred to me that I might want to get to know some of Elizabeth's relatives, and her heirs as well. The more I thought about it, the more I was convinced that I would have to know Elizabeth a lot better if I was going to be able to help Tom.

A quick glance at my watch told me that it would be dinnertime very shortly. I decided if I wanted to see who was staying here at the lodge, I might want to get down to the main room and watch them as they come for dinner. It would give me a chance to observe them before I actually met them.

Before I left my room, I made sure the door that joined the room next to mine was locked from my side. When I left my room, I also made sure I locked the door behind me before walking down the hall.

As I walked along the carpeted hall, I made it a point of listening for any unusual noises, either in the hall or coming from the rooms, but I heard nothing. The hall carpet was too thick and the rooms were quiet.

However, as I descended the stairs, I noticed that the third step from the top squeaked when I stepped on it. I made a mental note of it for possible future reference.

I stopped about halfway down the stairs and looked out over the main room. It was possible to see almost the entire room, from the doors that led into the dining room at one end, to the front door at the other end. The view of the entire room gave one a sense of its immense size.

As I looked down into the main room, I immediately noticed a young couple sitting on the far side of the room on a window bench. I guessed they were most likely newlyweds as they sat looking into each other's eyes while they held hands. They also sat so close together that their legs and hips were touching, and they seemed oblivious to everything in the room except each other. I smiled as I thought about how lucky they were to have each other.

As I continued to scan the room, I noticed two other people sitting just below me next to a small table. I couldn't see their faces, but it was clear that they were not newlyweds. They sat in chairs with the table between them and were not talking to each other. The man was slightly bald and dressed in a dark cardigan sweater, a dress shirt and gray dress slacks. The man seemed to be engrossed in a big city newspaper. From where I was standing, I could not tell what city the paper was from. However, I did notice that he was reading the business section of the paper.

The woman was wearing a dark purple dress that was simple, yet elegant for a woman of her size. I noticed streaks of gray in her hair indicating that she was not a young woman. The woman was busy reading a magazine.

The old man who had been sitting in one of the corners earlier was not in the room. I wondered where he might be. It was possible that he had already checked out of the lodge, but something in the back of my head caused me to think otherwise. It was probably the fact that he seemed so interested in me when I first checked in.

I did see the woman that had been on the front porch when I arrived. She was sitting on a sofa near the fireplace casually flipping through the pages of a woman's magazine. She slowly looked up. When she saw me, a very pleasant smile came over her face. She seemed rather pleased to see me again which I found encouraging.

I watched her for a second or two, until she motioned for me to come down and join her. It seemed like a good idea to me, so I went on down the stairs and crossed the room to her.

"Good evening," I said as I stopped and stood in front of her.

"Good evening. You looked like you could use some company," she replied with a big smile as she pointed to a place on the sofa next to her.

"Thank you."

I moved to the sofa and sat down next to her. The smile on her face was captivating, as well as the sparkle in those beautiful blue eyes. The sweater she had on now was very flattering to her and matched the color of her eyes.

"What brings you all the way out here on such a dreary day as this?" she asked, her voice having a very pleasant tone.

"I'm on vacation. What about you?"

"Well, this isn't actually a vacation for me, although it seems like one."

"I'm sorry. I don't understand," I said, a little confused by her answer.

"I'm doing research for the University of Wisconsin's History Department," she said softly.

"Oh, really. What are you researching?"

"The history of the area, and the history of this old house in particular," she said.

"You mean this lodge?"

"Yes, but a hundred years ago it was a private home," she said as she quickly glanced around the main room.

"I knew that. It once belonged to a Captain Bartholomew Samuelson. That's a portrait of him hanging above the fireplace," I said.

She would have had to be a complete dummy not to know who the man in the painting was. I only gave her that small token of information in the hope she might let me know what she had been able to find out about the lodge.

"That's correct. Did you know that Captain Samuelson built this house for himself and his young wife, Elizabeth?"

"Yes, I believe I'd heard that somewhere."

"Did you know that about one hundred years ago Captain Samuelson's wife disappeared and was never found?" she asked with a very pleasant smile.

I didn't bother to answer her question. She seemed to be interested in talking about the lodge. I figured that if I didn't say anything more, she might just tell me some of the background information that I hoped would be helpful to me later on.

"What makes this place so interesting," she continued, "is some of the local people think that she, Captain Samuelson's wife, was washed up on the beach in front of the lodge about three or four months ago."

"I think I read something about that in the paper. She was frozen in a large block of ice, if I remember correctly."

It was obvious by the look on her face that she was surprised I seemed to be so well informed. But before she could comment any further, we were interrupted by a call to dinner. She immediately stood up. I had already decided that it was entirely possible she could have some information that would help me find out what was going on here. However, my immediate problem was how to get her to willingly give up what information she knew without having to tell her why I was here in the first place.

"Would you care to sit with me at dinner?" she asked.

"I'd like that. By the way, my name is Nick, Nick McCord."

"Monica, Monica Barnhart," she replied with a smile.

"You wouldn't happen to be Professor Barnhart from the University of Wisconsin?"

"Yes," she answered with a big grin and then started into the dining room.

I knew from the Milwaukee newspapers that Professor M. Barnhart was well known for her knowledge of the history of Wisconsin. I was surprised to discover that the professor was not a short, overweight, wrinkled, old lady with gray hair, but rather a tall, slender, very well stacked, even sexy woman in her late twenties.

I gladly followed her into the dining room. I held out a chair for her and then sat down beside her. I took my time as I looked around the large dining room table observing everyone there.

The old man I had seen in the main room when I arrived was sitting at one end of the table. At the other end was my friend, Tom. Across the table was the young couple I had seen in the main room earlier.

Next to the young couple was the other couple that had been sitting at the bottom of the stairs in the main room. I was a little surprised to see that the man was much smaller than I had thought. He was a man of small stature with a sharp pointed chin and high sharp cheekbones, and a thin face. He wore wire-rimmed glasses that gave him a scholarly appearance. His deep set eyes were dark brown, almost black, and his thinning gray hair was neatly trimmed. The expression on his face was that of someone who wished they could be any place in the world, but here. He glanced up at me, but quickly looked away. I got the impression that he was afraid of something, but there was no telling just what it might be.

The woman sitting beside him, whom I guessed to be his wife, was a rather large woman with big bones and hard, well-defined features. She was a little overweight, but seemed to be able to carry it well on her large frame. Her build reminded me of the stereotype of a Russian peasant woman, strong and forceful.

However, the look in her eyes when she stared across the table at me sent a cold chill down my back. There was something about the woman that didn't set well with me. Maybe it was that she appeared to be a hard, possibly even ruthless, woman without any scruples.

My first thought was that I would not want to get the woman mad at me, or meet her alone in a dark alley. She looked as if she could kill a person without so much as blinking an eye or giving it a second thought.

Sitting to Monica's right were two other people who I had not seen before. I could not see them very well, but from what little I could see there appeared to be nothing exceptional about them. I did, however, catch the woman glancing across the table at the big woman from time to time. I couldn't say for sure, but I got the impression that they might very well know each other, but didn't want anyone else to know it.

After the food had been passed around the table, everyone immediately began to eat. It seemed kind of strange that no one seemed to want to talk. Usually in a lodge like this, everyone tries to get to know the others. They tell a little about themselves and ask the usual questions like where are you from, and what do you do for a living, but not here. I decided that I would take the bull by the horns and talk to the man across the table from me, the small man with the thin face.

"Hello, I'm Nick McCord. Who might you be, sir?"

The man had a fork full of meat that he was just about to put in his mouth. I must have startled him as he stopped suddenly and looked at me over the top of his fork, but didn't reply. The look in his eyes was that of a man who was scared, but scared of what I had no idea? It was as if talking to me was terribly frightening for him.

The woman looked at him, then at me. She looked at me as if I had done something horribly wrong, but must have decided that it was rude not to reply. Slowly, a forced smile came over her face. It was one of the phoniest smiles I'd seen in a very long time. It would have been better if she had not tried to smile at all.

"This is my husband, Mr. Arthur Mortimer," she said slowly and so politely that it almost made a person sick.

It was clear by the tone of her voice that she did not want to carry on any kind of lengthy conversation with me, or anyone else for that matter. As I looked around the table at the other guests, I noticed that they were all looking at me. I suddenly felt as if I had broken some secret vow of silence and that all hell and damnation was going to beset all of us.

It had apparently been made clear before I arrived that conversations at the dinner table were out of the question.

As soon as I looked down the table toward Tom, everyone stopped looking at me and returned to eating as if nothing had happened. Tom quickly looked down at his plate and began picking at his food. I watched him for a minute or so. It seemed to me that he was afraid to eat the food in front of him.

At this point, no one else in the room seemed to be paying any attention to me, or to anyone else. They all had returned to eating.

I glanced over at Monica and caught her watching me. She must have seen me looking at Tom. She appeared to be as puzzled by what had just happened as I was.

She leaned over close to me and whispered in my ear, "This is a strange place. No one ever talks at the table."

"So I've noticed," I whispered.

I didn't say anything more. The message had come through loud and clear. As I finished eating my dinner, I watched the others. As soon as the others had finished their meals, they simply left the table. No one waited for the other guests to finish.

As Mrs. Mortimer left the table with her husband, she turned and glared at me. Then the young couple left, followed by the old man. Before long, the only ones left at the table were Tom, Monica and I.

"Tom, are you all right?" I asked.

Tom looked around the room and at Monica. It was clear he was afraid to say anything that might be overheard.

"Can you tell me what the hell is going on here?" Monica asked. "I thought that a lodge like this would be a place where a person could come to relax and meet new people, but this place is, - - well, - - it's weird," she said as she gave a little shutter of her shoulders.

I couldn't have agreed with her more. This was not what one would expect at the typical vacation lodge. I wanted to know what was going on here, too.

Tom looked at me as if he were asking me for approval to speak in front of Monica. My gut feeling was that Monica was all right, but I wanted some kind of reassurance. But that was probably not in the cards at the moment. I decided to trust my gut feeling and accept Monica as I found her.

"Monica, when did you arrive here?"

"Just this morning, why?"

"I'll explain later.

"Tom, who's in the room next to mine?"

"I am," Monica answered, the look on her face showing she wondered why I wanted to know.

"You!"

"Yes. I have the room adjoining your room."

"Oh. No, I meant on the other side of my room."

"That would be the Thorndikes. They were the couple that was sitting next to you," Tom said as he looked at Monica.

The Thorndikes had not said anything all evening and I had not been able to watch them from where I was sitting. I had to wonder why they were acting as if they didn't know Mr. and Mrs. Mortimer when it had become clear to me that at least Mrs. Thorndike knew Mrs. Mortimer. I also wondered why the Thorndikes would have such an interest in me that they would talk about me in their room.

"Tom, what time do you usually shut things down and go to bed?"

"The place usually gets pretty quiet by about ten o'clock. That's about the time I turn down most of the lights and close up for the night," he explained.

"Tonight, I want you to do everything the same as you would on any other night. Don't change your routine," I said.

Tom looked at me as if he were wondering what I was up to, but agreed without comment. I could see by the expression on Monica's face that she was wondering what I had in mind, too.

"Monica, I know what I am going to ask you might sound strange to you, but I hope you will trust me. I would like you to meet me in my room after everything is quiet. I will explain it all then."

"That's one incredible line you have. I think I'll take you up on it just to find out where it goes from there," she replied with a grin.

I decided there was no need to say anything more right now. As long as she had agreed to come to my room, I could explain what little I knew and see if she could provide me with some more insight into the history of the place.

"Do you have any suggestions on what we can do until it's quiet?" she asked.

"How about a game of rummy in the main room?" I suggested.

"Okay, but be prepared to be beaten," she said with a sparkle in her eye.

I smiled at her and then stood up. I held her chair for her as she stood up. She wrapped her arm in mine and we walked out of the dining room and into the main room.

CHAPTER FOUR

Upon entering the main room of the lodge, Monica and I found a small table in a corner that would allow us almost a full view of the entire room. The table had an old fashion table lamp setting on it. At the base of the lamp was a neatly stacked deck of cards, a small score pad and a pencil. We sat down at the table and Monica picked up the deck of cards.

"A penny a point," she suggested with a smile.

"I'm game as long as you don't take too much of an advantage of me," I replied with a grin.

Monica grinned as she began to shuffle the cards and dealt out the first hand. I took the opportunity to look around the room to see who had stayed downstairs and who had gone somewhere else.

Tom had not come out into the main room at all. He had disappeared very shortly after dinner. I figured that he might have decided to go lay down. I couldn't blame him, as he looked extremely tired.

The Mortimers must have gone directly upstairs after leaving the dining room. They were not in the main room. The last time I saw them, Mrs. Mortimer had Arthur by the arm and was escorting him toward the stairs. I got the distinct impression that Arthur didn't really want to go upstairs, but was afraid to resist her.

The old man who had been sitting at the end of the table during dinner was not in the main room, either. I wondered where he had gone and what he was doing. The way he carried himself and the way he was dressed sort of reminded me of the undertakers like those I had seen in so many of the old western movies. The only difference was that his suit was very expensive and very nicely tailored. If I had to guess, it was probably an Armani suit. It was clear that money was not a problem for him. The expensive clothes said he had plenty of it, that, along with the high priced cars setting out front. The only thing about him that didn't seem to fit was the fact he appeared to be here alone.

The young newlywed couple did not stay in the main room very long. They had been sitting in a corner next to the window for a little while, but obviously they had better things to do than sit around with a bunch of old folks who had nothing better to do then to read magazines or play cards, so they went upstairs early. They seemed to be so wrapped up in each other that I doubted they were even aware there was anything wrong.

The Thorndikes had picked out a small table near the fireplace. They were playing some sort of card game that was not familiar to me. After watching them for a while I wasn't sure they were even playing a card game. Mr. Thorndike seemed to spend more time glancing at us over the top of the cards in his hands than he did looking at his cards. It was almost funny watching Mrs. Thorndike trying to pretend to look at her cards when all the time it was clear that she was looking over them. It was about eight-thirty when they finally gave up on us and retired to the upstairs.

Almost immediately after the Thorndikes retired, Mrs. Mortimer returned to the main room without Arthur. She sat down next to a small table with a reading lamp near the stairs. She pretended to read a magazine, but I noticed that she kept looking over the top of it to see what Monica and I were doing. After about an hour and a half of watching us, she must have decided that we weren't going to do anything interesting tonight. She finally gave up on us. She closed the magazine, laid it on the table and went back upstairs.

The only thing I found out this evening was that there were several people who seemed to take a great deal of interest in what I was doing there. That bit of information was of little help to me, at least for now. My only hope of finding out anything tonight was if Monica could shed some light on the background of the lodge. I didn't know what help that would be, but I had to start somewhere and it seemed to be as good a place as any at the moment.

Monica must have realized that I was not paying much attention to the game. She laid her cards on the table and looked up at me.

"If you don't mind, I think I will go upstairs. I'm kind of tired," she said.

"Okay."

"Will I see you later?" she asked in a whisper as she leaned close to me.

"Yes," I replied softly. "I want to wait and talk to Tom for a minute."

"Okay. Just knock when you get to your room."

I nodded in agreement and watched her as she walked across the room and up the stairs. She had been very pleasant company all evening even if she did beat me at rummy. I enjoyed her company very much and hoped that we might get to know each other better. The fact that she was a beautiful woman made getting to know her even more interesting.

I didn't have long to wait for Tom. It was shortly after ten when he came into the main room. He shut off several of the brighter lights as he walked across the room toward me.

"All quiet?" he asked as he glanced around the room.

"Seems to be," I replied.

"Has everyone gone to bed?"

"Well, they've gone upstairs, except for the old man."

"Where did he go?" Tom asked.

"I don't know. I was hoping that you could tell me."

"I don't know where he goes. Sometimes he leaves in his car and sometime he just goes for a walk along the shore.

"Well, he left shortly after dinner and I haven't seen him since. By the way, do you know who is he?"

"Sure. His name is Franklin J. Beresford. He is one of the wealthiest men I know. He's been staying here for several months now. Always pays his bill on time and never causes any trouble. In fact, I don't see him much except at meals. He's a very quiet man."

"You said he has been here for several months?"

"Yes," he replied.

"Isn't it a little strange for someone to stay that long?"

"Yes, but he seems to like it here. I don't know if he has any family."

"Just when did he get here?"

Tom must have seen the disturbed look on my face. He knew something was going on in my head.

"What are you getting at, Nick?"

"When did he get here?" I asked, avoiding his question.

Tom thought for a minute. Suddenly his eyes lit up like a light bulb and I was now sure that there was something going on in his head.

"He came just three days after Elizabeth Samuelson washed up on the beach. You think he might have something to do with what's going on around here?"

"It's possible, but hard to tell."

I couldn't see what the connection could be between the old man and the woman who washed up on the beach, but the fact he arrived here so quickly after the incident, and that he had been here for so long, made me wonder about him. There was always the possibility that he was connected with what had been happening to Tom, but at this point I had no idea what it might be. I was beginning to think that it might be a good idea to start up a conversation with Mr. Beresford. There's no telling what he might say, or what might slip out if I could get him to talk at all. A look into his background might also be in order.

"Do you know if the Mortimers and the Thorndikes know each other?" I asked.

Tom seemed to think for a moment before answering.

"They could, but I don't think so."

Maybe I was on the wrong track, but I couldn't get the idea that they knew each other, and probably knew each other well, out of my head. Maybe I was reading too much into the way Mrs. Thorndike and Mrs. Mortimer looked at each other at the dinner table.

As best I could tell, there was nothing more that Tom could help me with tonight. He looked very tired and it would probably be a good idea for him to turn in for the night.

"Tom, I think you should go to bed. You look tired. I'll visit with you tomorrow."

He nodded his head in agreement, said goodnight, turned and walked away. I watched him as he disappeared into the dining room.

There certainly was something very strange about the lodge and the people who were staying here, I thought as I stood there a few minutes thinking.

My thoughts quickly turned to Monica. I hoped that she was still waiting for me to knock on her door. I wasn't sure just what I was going to tell her or what she could tell me, but I was hoping that with her knowledge of local history, she might be able to provide me with a little information on Captain Samuelson and his young wife that might be helpful.

I turned and started up the stairs. I had only gone about halfway up the stairs when I heard a noise at the front door. I stopped and stepped back into the shadows. I watched as the front door of the lodge opened and in walked Mr. Beresford. He came into the main room and started walking across the room, stopping suddenly near the center of the room. He looked around as if he sensed that someone might be watching him. I thought about saying something to him, but decided better of it. I was sure that he could not see me, and I was very much interested in seeing what he was going to do.

When he seemed to be convinced that no one was around to see him, he turned and walked over to the fireplace. He put one hand on the mantel and leaned forward. He had his back to me so I could not see what he was doing, but it looked as if he took something from his pocket and tossed it into the fireplace. It appeared to be a piece of paper as it flared up and died down rather quickly on the red-hot coals of the fire, but I couldn't be sure.

Since he still had his back to me, I figured it was a good time to go on upstairs without being noticed and before he decided to come upstairs. As I moved up the steps, I remembered that the third step from the top would squeak if I were to step on it. I carefully stepped over it and quickly moved around the corner into the hall, out of sight. I hurried on down the dimly lit hall to my room, unlocked my door and entered.

As I closed the door behind me, I got the feeling that something was not right. I turned on the light and slowly looked around the room. At first glance, the room appeared to be just as I had left it. Everything was in its place and my suitcase was still tightly closed. Then it came to me with the suddenness of a bolt of lighting. Everything was not just as I had left it.

Someone had been in my room and had gone though my suitcase. I noticed my suitcase was closed and zipped shut. When I had left the room earlier, I had simply shut the top down and zipped up only the sides of the suitcase leaving the front open. I had not zipped it completely shut as it was now.

I opened my suitcase and examined the contents very carefully. Someone had rummaged around in my suitcase all right, but why? I didn't have anything in it that would be of interest to anyone else. All I had in the suitcase were my clothes and a few personal items, nothing anyone would want. I didn't even have any identification in it, as I didn't want anyone to find out who I was before I was ready to let them know. I had left my gun and my Milwaukee Police Department identification locked in a steel box in the trunk of my car under an old blanket.

I remembered that Monica was waiting for me to knock on our adjoining doors. My first thought was that Monica might have gone through my suitcase. But for some reason I couldn't explain, that thought didn't seem logical.

I closed the top on the suitcase and quietly opened my side of the adjoining doors. I lightly tapped on her side of the doors and she opened it almost immediately. She stood there and smiled up at me.

"I thought you might have forgotten about me."

"How could I forget you," I said as I looked at her.

She was wearing a very lacy nightgown with a deep cut neckline under a fitted velvet robe. The robe was tied at her waist accenting her full firm breasts, narrow waist and the smooth lines of her hips. The exposed skin from her neck down between her breasts looked soft and creamy.

"Come in," I whispered.

I stepped back as she stepped into my room. She looked around the room, then turned back to face me. She was about to say something, but stopped when she saw me with a finger over my mouth.

"These walls have ears," I whispered. "I can hear some of what goes on in the next room."

She nodded her head to let me know that she understood. Monica moved as gracefully as a swan as she crossed the room to the bed and sat down on the edge. She patted the bed next to her and I joined her on the bed, sitting down beside her.

"Do you know what is going on around here?" she asked softly.

The tone of her voice and the look in her eyes convinced me that she was not a part of anything that was happening here. It was also clear that she wanted answers to some very disturbing questions as much as I did.

"No. Has anyone been in your room?"

"Yes," she replied softly. "Why do you ask?"

"Someone went through my suitcase this evening."

"Mine, too."

I still wasn't totally convinced I should share everything that I knew about this place with her, but I needed her help. If I was going to get her help, I would have to trust her and ask her for help. I happened to know that Professor Monica Barnhart had a reputation for being a fair and honest person. I only hoped that it carried over to Monica Barnhart.

"I'm going to trust you with some information that I do not want to leave this room. Can I trust you to keep it between us?" I asked in a whisper.

"Sure," she replied with a keen interest in what I was about to tell her.

"Tom Walker is a very good friend of mine. He asked me to come up here to see if I could figure out why he is seeing strange things and hearing strange noises at night," I explained.

Her eyes showed her excitement as she thought about what I had said.

"You mean, like ghosts?"

"I don't know if I would call them 'ghosts', but someone apparently wants him to think he is seeing and hearing ghosts. I don't know if you noticed, but Tom looks tired and appears to be much older then I am. Tom and I are the same age."

"You're kidding," she said with a look of surprise.

"No. In fact, he is three months younger than I am. I think someone is trying to drive him crazy, or at least trying to drive him out of the lodge."

"So you're here to find his ghosts?" she asked keeping her voice low.

"Sort of, but I think there is much more to it than a ghost. I believe that someone, a real person, is trying to get control of his lodge. My problem is that I don't know who, and I don't know why. It apparently started when a body encased in a large block of ice was supposed to have washed up on the beach in front of the lodge."

Monica looked at me with surprise. I could see in her eyes that she wanted to tell me something.

"I came here to investigate some of the rumors about that very thing. There are apparently some people who believe the body in the ice was that of Elizabeth Samuelson, the young wife of Bartholomew Samuelson. There are some others who don't think it is Elizabeth. From what the police records indicate, the body has yet to be identified," she explained.

"You've seen the police records?"

"Yes."

Needless to say, I was surprised that she had seen the police records. Most of the time, the police are very careful about what information they give out on cases they still considered open.

"Do you have access to those records?" I asked.

"Sure," she replied casually. "It was the police who asked the University for some background information on Elizabeth Samuelson, Bartholomew Samuelson and the lodge. I did the original background checks, at least as much of it as I could from the university. Apparently there was nothing of any use to them in my report. I came up here for a few days hoping that I might get some insight and additional background information."

"What do you mean there was nothing of any use?"

"It seems the police couldn't find any solid evidence that it was, in fact, Elizabeth Samuelson entombed in the block of ice. Nor could they figure out what was the cause of death. As far as I know, it is still considered just another unsolved death, nothing more," she explained.

"There appears to be more to it than that, a lot more," I insisted.

"Oh, I agree, but what?"

"I don't know yet. Do you have the police reports with you?" I asked, knowing that it was a long shot.

"I have copies of the reports in my room. I'll get them," Monica said as she stood up.

I stood up and watched Monica as she returned to her room. I was hoping that the police reports would be able to give me a clue, or at least a place to start looking for answers. Monica returned with a large envelope and handed it to me.

"I hope this helps," she whispered as she handed me the envelope.

"Me, too," I replied as I took the envelope from her.

Monica returned to the bed and sat down while I emptied the contents of the envelope onto the small desk. I pulled up a chair, sat down and turned on the light on the desk.

I went over each piece of paper being very careful not to miss anything that might be important. I reviewed each officer's report, the autopsy report and the lab reports. The only things that seemed to be conclusive was that the dead woman had been dead a very long time, but apparently it had been impossible for them to determine just how long.

The autopsy and lab reports proved to be the most interesting. The lab reports indicated that there were no poisons used in the death of the woman. There hadn't been any signs of violence on the body such as gunshot wounds, stab wound, and no signs of strangulation, nothing. There was also nothing to indicate that she died of some disease. In short, there was no reason for the woman to have died at such a young age. However, the autopsy report indicated that the woman could have been dead for as little as twenty years or as long as a hundred years or more.

On the surface, the reports did not appear to be of much help. I was a little surprised that the lab was unable to determine how long the woman had been dead with at least a little more accuracy. Considering the small town police lab, that shouldn't have been all that great a surprise. However, the reports did indicate that there was a slim possibility the body was that of Elizabeth Samuelson, but it could not be proven.

I had to admit that the reports caused more questions than they answered. The reports did reassure me that Tom might have had good reason to believe that the body was Elizabeth's. The one real question that kept haunting me was how was it possible that her body could surface on the beach after so many years and still be in such good condition? I could come up with but one answer. She would have had to have been frozen in the block of ice for over a hundred years, and then placed on the beach, probably during the night, so Tom would find it on his usual morning walk along the shore. There was no way she could have "washed up" on the beach.

"That's it," I said as I turned around to Monica.

I smiled as I looked at her curled up on my bed. She must have been very tired to fall asleep while I examined the reports. Glancing at my watch, I saw that it was well past two in the morning. It was no wonder she was tired.

She was sleeping so soundly that I didn't have the heart to wake her. What I had discovered from the reports could wait until morning.

I turned back around and gathered up the reports. After neatly putting them back in the envelope and sealing it, I went over to the bed. I took a quilt off the foot of the bed and covered her with it. I then carefully laid down on the bed beside her in the hope of not disturbing her.

Even though it was late, I could not just close my eyes and fall asleep. There were too many unanswered questions running through my mind. I lay there for sometime staring at the ceiling.

Monica stirred, then rolled over against me, putting her head on my shoulder and her arm across my chest. I wrapped my arm around her and held her close. I felt very content lying there with her. It had been a long day for both of us, and it was not long before I was asleep, too.

CHAPTER FIVE

I wasn't sure what it was that woke me, but I suddenly became very conscious to my surroundings. It could have been the sun shining through a small opening in the drapes of the long narrow windows, or possibly the feel of the beautiful woman lying beside me who stirred slightly as she snuggled up against me. It could have even been a sound from somewhere in the lodge that stirred my senses. Whatever it was, I was awake and listening carefully to see if my neighbors in the next room were up and about, but I heard nothing.

I didn't want to move, as Monica seemed to be sleeping soundly, but I needed to get up. As quietly as possible, I rolled over to the edge of the bed and swung my legs over the side. I sat up and rubbed the sleep from my eyes.

"Mmmm, Good morning," Monica whispered softly as she rolled over on her back and stretched.

"Good morning to you, too," I replied as I looked back over my shoulder at her lying on my bed.

I took a few seconds to admire the smooth flowing lines of her body stretched out behind me. I couldn't remember ever seeing a woman who looked so lovely after just waking up.

"Did you find anything in the reports that would help you?"

"Yes, as a matter of fact I did, and in the most unlikely place, too."

"You did! What?" she asked excitedly as she sat up.

I held my finger against my lips to quickly remind her that the walls were very thin and it would be best if we spoke softly.

"It was not so much what the reports said as what they didn't say."

"I don't understand?" she whispered, looking a little confused.

"The reports indicated that the body incased in the ice was well preserved. It also said that the woman had been dead for at least twenty years, and possibly as long as a hundred years or more.

"That's right. I read the report," Monica said, still looking a little confused.

"First of all, Lake Michigan doesn't freeze over completely every year, and what ice does form on the lake always melts by spring or early summer at the latest. It would be impossible for a body not to completely decompose under such conditions over such a long period of time.

"For the body to be so well preserved, it would have had to have been kept frozen solid at a pretty constant temperature all year round. That just can't happen in the lake."

Monica gave some thought to what I had said before she responded.

"So the body had to have been hidden someplace where it would be very cold all year around. Someplace where it would remain frozen all the time," she said as she looked at me.

"Right," I agreed. "But, now we have some more questions to answer. Where had the body been for the past hundred years or more, assuming that it is Elizabeth? Who hid the body? And of course, who found it?"

"Somebody would have had to put the body on the beach just before it was found if they wanted it to be found by Tom. It was probably put on the beach during the night when no one would be around to see it being done," Monica added.

"True. The big questions are who put the body on the beach? And, of course, why?"

"If we could figure out the answer to where the body had been kept all those years, we might be able to figure out the answers to some of the other questions, don't you think?" she asked.

"We might," I agreed. "And I just might have the answer to that question," I said with a grin.

"Which one?"

"The one about where the body had been kept."

"Where?" she asked as she straightened up.

"When I was in my late teens, I spent some time in upper Michigan exploring some of the old copper mines with my brother. One of the things we discovered was that a lot of the old mines still had ice down inside them, even in late August and early September. An old mine might be just the place to hide a body for over a hundred years," I suggested.

Monica looked a little confused. "I thought that the deeper the mine, the warmer it got, at least to a point?"

"That's true in really deep mines. But there are a number of mines around here that don't go very deep, retaining the cold winter temperatures all year round.

"How would you like to go into Sturgeon Bay with me?" I asked.

"Sure, but what for?" she replied.

"We should be able to find an old map of this area in the county courthouse. Most of the old county maps had the locations of mines shown on them. It might just tell us if there are any old mines that are close to the lodge, or in the immediate area."

I could see by the excited expression on her face that this was going to be like a treasure hunt to her. I'm afraid that I took it to be much more than a simple treasure hunt. I was not interested in gold, silver or jewels. I was looking for some answers to questions that could mean the difference between life and death for my friend.

Monica smiled and slid off the bed with the ease and grace of a woman with style. She turned, looked at me and said, "I'll meet you downstairs in a little while."

"Be sure to wear something comfortable," I reminded her. "We might have a lot of walking to do."

I watched her as she left through the adjoining door and disappeared into her room, closing the door behind her. I stood up and closed the door on my side.

My mind quickly filled with thoughts about the death of Elizabeth Samuelson. It seemed strange that the police lab had failed to come up with a cause of death.

I turned and went into the bathroom to shave. It gave me time to think, and to remember that this little county sheriff's office would not have the resources that a big city police department would have available to it. That could explain the reason that the reports were so unclear. Yet, they would have the state police labs to help them if they just thought to ask. I had seen nothing in the report that would indicate they had asked for help from the state police labs.

I changed into a comfortable pair of slacks and sport shirt for the trip into town. Just as I was about to leave my room, I heard the door to the room next to mine open and then close. I quickly moved over next to the wall in the hope of hearing something that might give me a lead, a clue, anything that would be of help in discovering what was going on here. I stood very quietly near the wall and listened for any conversation my neighbors might have. I could barely hear them. However, I was able to make out most of what was being said at first.

"I think he's on to us, Elinor. Did you see the way he watched every move I made last night? He's going to find out about us and what we're doing here."

"Oh for Christ sake, Priscilla, pull yourself together and keep your voice down before you ruin everything. I knew Andrew should have left you back in Chicago where he found you. Nothing. Nothing is going to ruin what I have spent years planning. Not you and certainly not this man, whoever he is. Do you understand that?"

That was the last of their conversation I was able to hear. From that point on, all I could hear was some mumbling that I could not understand. I sat down on the edge of my bed to think for a minute.

This was the first time that I had heard any of them use their first names. I couldn't be sure who one of the voices belonged to, but I was sure that I recognized one as Mrs. Mortimer. If I was correct, her name was Elinor, Elinor Mortimer.

If my thinking was correct, then there was a strong possibility that the other voice was that of Mrs. Thorndike, Mrs. Priscilla Thorndike. If it was Priscilla Thorndike, she was extremely nervous and frightened that I might find out something, but what? I didn't have the vaguest idea of what she thought I might find.

I was sure they were talking about me, and I began to remember last night at the dinner table. Priscilla Thorndike had not said a word during the entire meal, but I noticed that she kept looking across the table at Elinor as if she was looking for direction, or maybe it was reassurance she was looking for, I thought.

Thinking back to the time spent in the main room after dinner, the Thorndikes had been watching us. They left the room when Elinor came down from the second floor. It hadn't occurred to me at the time, but now that I thought about it, it was almost like the changing of the guard. The Thorndikes were keeping an eye on us while Elinor put her husband to bed and went through our luggage. Then Elinor came down to the main room so the Thorndikes could go up to their room. It made perfect sense and it all fit together. The only problem I had was for what reason?

The comment about "he's on to us" gave me reason to pause and to ponder. I was certain they were talking about me, but what was she afraid I'd found out, or might find out? Up until now, all I had was a bunch of unanswered questions, none of which had pointed to them, until now.

The mumbling stopped, and then I heard the door open and close again. Then after a moment or two, I heard the door on the other side of my room open and close. That would mean that Monica was on her way downstairs. I decided to wait a couple of minutes before I went downstairs to meet her.

I glanced around my room. The police reports were still lying on the desk in the envelope. Someone had already been in my room and searched it. I didn't want to take any chances that the reports would be found in my room if it was searched again. It seemed to me that a secure place for them would be in my suitcase that had already been gone through, by whom I still wasn't a hundred percent sure.

Then it occurred to me that, if Monica's luggage had been searched, there was a good chance that whoever did the searching had already seen the police reports and most likely knew what was in them.

After placing the reports in among my shirts, I went to the door. I took one long, last look around the room, then stepped out into the hall and locked the door. I looked up and down the hall. It was empty.

As I started down the stairs, I made a point to look out over the main room to see who was around. Arthur and Elinor Mortimer were trying very hard to act as if they didn't know I was coming down the stairs. Andrew Thorndike was glancing at me over the top of his newspaper. For some reason, I found it interesting that Priscilla Thorndike was nowhere around. There was no one else in the room.

I made it a point to look directly at Elinor, smile and give her a slight nod. My acknowledgment of her watching me was greeted with a cold, hard stare. It was clear to me that this woman did not like me being there.

I didn't see Monica in the main room so I stepped out onto the porch and looked around. The sun was shining, and it was going to be a very warm and clear day. I found Monica was waiting for me in the little red sports car. She had put the top down.

"Are you going into town, Mr. McCord?" she called out.

I assumed that she was being so formal because someone might be watching us. I decided that it would be best to play along, just in case.

"Yes, are you?"

"Yes. Would you like to ride along?"

"Thank you, I'd enjoy the company."

I stepped down off the porch and crossed the lawn. As soon as I got in the car, she backed out of her parking spot.

"I wasn't sure, but I think there was someone in one of the towers watching us. I thought it might be best if it didn't look like we knew each other very well," Monica explained.

"Good thinking. It must have been Priscilla Thorndike. I noticed that she wasn't in the main room with her husband."

"It could have been, but I don't think so," Monica said as she pulled away from the lodge. "It looked like it might have been a man, but I didn't get a very good look. It might not have been a person at all, maybe a reflection of something."

Her comment opened a new train of thought for me. The only men I knew of who were not in the main room, were Franklin Beresford, the newlywed fellah and Tom Walker. Of course there was always the possibility that there was someone else in the house that I didn't know about. I made a mental note to ask Tom about the tower rooms and who had access to them when we returned to the lodge.

The little sports car purred along the road with the same smoothness and grace as its owner had shown in my room. I looked over at her and watched the wind blow through her soft, shiny hair.

Monica glanced over at me and smiled. She quickly turned back to watch the road.

"You said that someone had gone through your luggage last night?" I asked.

She glanced my way and replied, "That's right."

"Is it possible that whoever went through our luggage saw the police report?"

"It's possible, but I don't think so. I had the reports in my briefcase and it was leaning against the side of my bed. Whoever was in my room would probably not have seen my briefcase. It was on the other side of the bed, out of sight. It didn't look like it had been disturbed," she explained.

"Good," I replied as I sat back to enjoy the ride.

It was about a forty mile drive to Sturgeon Bay. We spent the rest of the drive enjoying the scenery and the fresh air. When we arrived in town, we went directly to the courthouse and to the record office. The young clerk at the desk introduced us to a Miss McGaughey, an older lady who I found out had worked in the record section of the courthouse for over thirty years.

After I told her what we were interested in, she directed us to the old maps of the county. She seemed to know the county history very well.

As I studied the old county maps, I discovered that there had been an old mine not very far from the lodge. In fact, there were two mines that looked as if they might be rather close to the lodge. From the looks of the locations on the map, one was probably on the lodge's property.

I began to think about preserving food during the summer and thought that there must have been some provisions made for the storage of food back when the house was originally built. I remembered that in the old days, back before refrigeration, they used to go out on ponds and lakes during the winter, and cut large blocks of ice out of the ponds. They would put the ice in icehouses where it would keep food cold for all or most of the summer, depending on the summer.

"Did you find what you are looking for, Mr. McCord?" Miss McGaughey asked when she came to check on us.

"Yes, thank you. Say, I was wondering if some of these old houses might have had some kind of icehouse or cold cellar as a place to store food?"

"Oh, yes," she replied. "Most of the old houses built back before electricity and refrigerators had icehouses. Several of the larger houses owned by the very rich had icehouses that were connected directly to the house, usually by a short tunnel from the basement.

"We often get a lot of snow out here on the point. A tunnel made it easier to get into the icehouse in the winter," she said clearly as if she knew what she was talking about.

I found her response very interesting and wanted more information.

"These icehouses, could they keep large blocks of ice all summer?"

"Oh, I don't think so. Most of them would keep things cool and some would keep ice for most of the summer, but it was unlikely that they could keep ice all summer. It might be possible if it was a very short, cool summer," she added.

"Would it be possible to keep ice in, say one of these old mines?" I asked as I pointed to the locations of the mines on the map on the table.

"Oh, my, yes. Most of those old mines are full of ice. Mind you, you might have to go back in a ways to find it."

"Is it possible that there are mines out on the point that are not on this map?" I asked.

"It's possible, I guess. But they would have to be mines that were never registered for one reason or another."

"Miss McGaughey, you are a treasure."

My comment seemed to embarrass her, but she had no idea how much help she had been. I got a photocopy of the part of the old map that included the area around and near the lodge from the clerk. There were only three old copper mines indicated on the map, but at least it was a place to start. I knew that there was always the possibility that Elizabeth's body had been stored somewhere else, but my gut feeling told me that she had been close to the lodge.

I took Monica by the arm and led her out of the courthouse. When we reached the street, I paused and looked up at the sky. It was clear and the sun was warm, a much better looking day then yesterday had been. It was also about noon.

"How about some lunch?" I suggested.

"Sounds good. We missed breakfast," she said with a knowing smile.

Sturgeon Bay was a small town of about nine thousand, but it had a lot of tourist businesses. There were several small cafes within sight of the courthouse. However, there was one that quickly caught my attention. There was nothing really special about the café except that it looked as if it had been around for a long time. It looked comfortable, like an old pair of shoes, and it struck me as the place where the local old-timers might spend a lot of their day watching the tourists and talking over coffee.

"How about that place?" I said as I pointed to the café.

Monica looked at the café I pointed to and then looked at me as if I had no class at all.

"Are you sure you want to risk eating in there? It doesn't look all that clean."

"I have a feeling that café is where all the locals gather to discuss what's happening in the world, and in Sturgeon

Bay. Never know what we might be able to find out in a place like that," I said with a smile.

Monica was one very bright young woman. She immediately understood what I was getting at, and she was more then willing to go along with me. She took me by the arm and we started off toward the café.

My experience had taught me that it is sometimes very hard to get the locals to talk to strangers. But, if you show a mild interest in them, they will often tell you more than you really want to know. It doesn't hurt if you have a good-looking woman on your arm, too.

As we walked in the door, I did a quick survey of the place. The fixtures were old, but they were clean. It looked as if the walls could use a fresh coat of paint and the floor some new tile. The booths that lined two of the walls were the old wooden booths with high straight backs that made for a slight degree of privacy and limited your view of what was going on in the other parts of the café. There were several round wooden tables out in the center of the room with faded red and white checked plastic tablecloths.

I picked out an empty booth near the corner where we could see the others in the café and sat down. The menus were on the tables, sandwiched between the salt and peppershakers and the sugar dispenser. It wasn't long before a young high school aged girl arrived at the table to take our order. We ordered sandwiches and coffee and looked around the café while we waited for our food.

"What do you hope to gain by coming here?" Monica asked softly after the waitress left.

"I'm hoping to find someone who has lived here a long time, and knows the area exceptionally well. That old man sitting at the end of the counter looks like a man I would like to start up a conversation with."

The old man was wearing a pair of faded bib overalls with a long sleeved flannel shirt. He had on a pair of work boots that had seen better days. He had white hair that was trimmed short on the sides. His hands looked clean and were wrapped around a white mug with coffee in it. He looked comfortable right where he was sitting.

Monica looked over at the man. From the expression on her face, I could tell she was wondering why I picked him out of the four or five other old men sitting around the cafe. I watched her for a moment or two as she studied him.

She turned and looked at me.

"Okay, why him? What's so special about him?"

"First of all, he has been here all morning. He probably spends the better part of the morning right there on that stool."

"How do you know that?" she asked as she looked at him.

"He takes sugar in his coffee and the sugar dispenser in front of him is low, a good indication that he has had several cups of coffee already. Notice that all the rest of the sugar dispensers in the room are full.

"Also, look at the mud on the floor from his boots. Its spread all around his feet, and it's dry. He has been sitting in that same spot for a long time. The shifting of his feet has spread the mud around a little."

She smiled as she shook her head. "Okay, but what makes you think he knows the area better than the others?"

"He's very comfortable here. That would indicate that there's a very good chance that he has lived around here for sometime."

"Okay," she conceded. "How do you plan to get him over here?"

"That's the easy part. I'll simply tell him we would like some information about the history of the area."

"What makes you so sure he will come over here and talk to us?" she asked, convinced that it would not be all that easy for me to get him to talk to us.

"Have you been watching him?" I asked with a grin.

"Well, sort of, but not really," she admitted.

"I have. He seems to like to talk, and he has been watching us ever since we came in. It might be more appropriate to say he has been watching you. He knows a good-looking woman when he sees one," I said with a wink and then I stood up.

I walked across the room, introduced myself to the old man and invited him to join us. He didn't hesitate one second. He picked up his cup and followed me to the booth.

"Monica, this is Wilber Polk."

"Hi, Wilber," she said with a smile.

Wilber slid into the booth next to Monica. It was easy to see that Wilber did not mind sitting next to such a beautiful woman. When our meals came, we offered to buy Wilber lunch, but he just asked for a refill of his coffee cup.

We spent the next hour and a half talking to him. Wilber was a very willing talker and he seemed to know a lot about the area and its history. He even told us a little about the legend of Captain Samuelson which seemed to be a great part of the local color.

After leaving Wilber in the cafe, we headed back toward the lodge. While Monica drove, I spent most of the time trying to digest all the information that Wilber had provided, along with what I already knew about the area.

CHAPTER SIX

We arrived back at the lodge around one-thirty in the afternoon. During the drive back, I spent a good part of the time carefully studying the map we had gotten at the courthouse for the location of the mine that would be closest to the lodge.

If my estimates were correct, one of the old mines was within a few hundred feet of the lodge and another was less than a quarter of a mile away. The one that was closest to the lodge appeared to be only a short distance from the beach. However, I knew that these maps were often not as accurate as they appeared.

It seemed strange to me that a mine would be located so close to the beach. It was my guess that a mine this far out on the peninsula would probably be rather shallow, otherwise it would be full of water or ice. Yet a fairly shallow mine was just what we were looking for. It was more likely to have ice in it.

Monica pulled up in front of the lodge and parked the car. I quickly folded up the map so that no one would be able to see it. I also remembered what Monica had said when we left, so I glanced up toward the top windows of the tower to the left side of the porch. I didn't see anyone in any of the windows, but I did notice that the curtains on the top floor window was moving slightly as if someone had almost been caught peeking out, or as if there was a slight draft in the tower. This was an old house and there was a very strong possibility that the towers were a bit drafty.

Within a few seconds the curtains stopped moving which gave me reason to believe that it had not been a draft causing the curtains to move. But since I had not seen anything, I had no way of knowing for sure. I would take a minute to talk to Tom about the towers when no one else was around.

I quickly glanced over at the tower on the right, but saw nothing that would indicate that someone was in that tower. I looked over at Monica as she turned and looked toward me. It was clear that she was thinking the same thing I was.

"Did you see it?" she asked.

"I saw something move up there, but I'm not sure what. I think I better have a talk with Tom."

The look on Monica's face told me that she had something on her mind, so I listened very carefully to what she had to say.

"I don't want to sound, ah, cynical, but do you think Tom will give you straight answers to your questions?"

Her question startled me for a second. It had not occurred to me that Tom would lie to me, that he would call me to come up here to intentionally get me involved in something of his own doing. But on the other hand, Tom had changed a great deal in the past few years. For a second, I wondered if he was still the same Tom that I had known for so many years.

"Tom and I have been friends a long time, I would like to believe that he would tell me the truth," I said as I looked into Monica's eyes.

Monica nodded her head in understanding, but the look in her eyes told me that she wasn't so sure that I should dismiss Tom from being involved so quickly. I had to wonder if she might be right. I found it a little distasteful to think that Tom might have called me to come all this way just to lie to me. But on the other hand, if I was to keep an open mind, I had to include Tom as a possible party to whatever it was that was going on here.

"You have a good point," I had to admit. "I think it would be a good idea to keep whatever we find out to ourselves until we're sure of the extent of everyone's involvement. And that includes Tom."

"I didn't mean it to sound like I don't trust your friend," she said apologetically.

"That's okay. I can't let my friendship with him cloud my judgment. It is best to keep all avenues open until proven otherwise," I said with a smile in the hope that she would not feel too bad.

Monica looked up at the lodge, then back at me. "Now what do we do?" she asked.

"How about finding yourself a pair of jeans or something that you wouldn't mind getting dirty. We're going exploring."

"In the mines?" she asked excitedly.

"In the mines, that is if we can find them," I said with a smile.

The idea of going out and searching for the truth seemed to excite her. Maybe it was the idea of possibly finding some hidden treasure that excited her, but the truth somehow seemed to be what she would want to know more than the possibility of lost treasure.

Monica was interested in what happened here over a hundred years ago. I was more interested in what had happened in just the past few months and in what was happening now.

However, I was gradually becoming convinced that if I was going to get the answers I needed to solve the problems now, it would be necessary for me to get answers to some of the unresolved questions of the past. I could not get it out of my head that there was a very strong connection between the two.

"By the way, do you have a flashlight?" I asked.

"I have two in the trunk. Do you want me to get them?"

"No. Not now. Do they both work?"

"Yes, I think so."

"Good. We will need them if we can find the mines."

"Do you think we will have trouble finding the mines," she asked with a worried look on her face.

"These old maps are not always as accurate as they could be. It might turn out that the mines are not where the map indicates that they are," I explained.

"Oh," she replied.

"Shall we go in and change?"

"Sure," she said as she opened the car door.

I opened the car door on my side and got out of the car. She joined me in front of the car and we walked up the steps onto the front porch together. Just as I was about to reach for the doorknob, I stopped and took a quick look around to see if anyone was watching us. I didn't see anyone around.

"Meet me in the main room after you've changed," I suggested. "I want to find Tom and have a little talk with him."

Monica agreed before we went inside. She went on upstairs while I went through the dining room and into the kitchen to find Tom.

I found Tom sitting at a table in the kitchen with a bunch of papers laid out in front of him. He looked like he was working on orders of some kind, probably for supplies for the lodge.

"Excuse me, Tom, but do you have a minute to talk?"

Tom looked up from his work and motioned for me to join him. He pushed the papers together as I sat down on a chair across from him.

"What's on your mind, Nick? Have you found anything?"

"Not yet. I'd like to talk to you about the towers."

"Okay. What about them?"

"I was wondering, is anyone renting or possibly living on the top floor of either of the towers?"

"You mean the towers in the front? No," he replied with a very curious look on his face.

"Would anyone have access to them?"

"The only access to them would be either through room eight for the east side tower, or through my apartment for the other tower. The top floors of the towers are a story higher than the rest of the house. I didn't remodel them because it would be too expensive for the amount of room that could be gained. What's this about?" he asked.

"I think I saw someone in the west tower."

"Are you sure it was the top floor?"

"Yes, the very top floor."

"That's impossible. The only way to get into that part of the tower is through the level just below, the third floor. To get to that part of the west tower, you have to go through my apartment," he explained.

"There's no other way into the top floor of the west tower?" I asked as I started to wonder what it was that I saw up there.

"No. Wait, if I remember correctly there was an opening from the east tower into the attic, but you would have to almost crawl through the attic to get to the other tower. There isn't enough room to stand up in there," Tom explained.

"How would you get into the attic?"

"You would have to go into the tower from room eight, then go up through the opening in the ceiling to the third floor, then to the fourth floor of the tower and from there into the attic."

I thought about what he had said for a moment, then asked, "Is there anyone renting room eight?"

"No. That room is currently vacant."

"Is it locked?"

"Certainly. I always keep unused rooms locked."

"Could someone get up to the third floor of the tower once they were inside room eight?" I asked.

"I suppose they could, but they would need a ladder to get up there. There's no stairway any more," Tom added. "I took it out when I remodeled."

"Thanks," I said as I continued to think about the towers.

I nodded at Tom to indicate that I understood what he had told me and then I stood up to leave. As I walked through the kitchen toward the dining room, I wondered which one of the guests was getting into room eight and then on up into the attic. As I reached out to push the door to the dining room open, I stopped and turned around.

"Tom, do you know if any of the guests have been on the third floor?"

"No. They would have no reason to go up there. The whole top floor is my apartment, besides the door at the top of the stairs is always locked," he insisted.

Tom answered my questions all right, but if no one except Tom had access to the third floor, or room eight, then who was that in the window? The most logical answer, of course, was Tom. I have found that what is the most logical answer to a question is often the right answer. I hoped that in this case it was not the right answer.

As I thought about it, I had to wonder if Tom would have had time to get down from the west tower to the kitchen before I got to the kitchen. There were only three possible answers. Either Tom was lying to me about having someone else up there, or someone had found a way to get into the tower without Tom knowing about it, or Tom had a way to get from the tower to the kitchen without going through the hallways.

I went up the stairs to the second floor and turned to go down the hall. I stopped long enough to look up the stairs to the third floor. Sure enough, there was a door at the top of the stairs and it was closed. I thought about going up to the top of the stairs to see if it was locked, but decided against it.

Instead, I went to my room to change clothes. Monica would be waiting for me. I changed into jeans and a long sleeved shirt that would be good for exploring old mines.

Just as I was ready to leave my room, I heard a soft, muffled knock on the door. I hesitated just for a second before opening the door. Thinking that it might be Monica, I opened the door and started to speak to her, but stopped before I let a single word escape my lips. It was not Monica.

"I would like to talk to you, Mr. McCord. In private, if you don't mind."

Needless to say, I was astonished to see Mr. Beresford standing at my door. He looked rather nervous and I got the impression that he not only wanted to talk to me privately, he did not want anyone to see us talking, either.

"Come in, please," I said quietly as I stepped aside.

As he moved by me, I quickly checked the hall to see if anyone had seen him come in. I saw no one, so I quickly ducked back inside my room and closed the door. When I turned around, I found that Mr. Beresford had already crossed my room and was seated in one of the chairs. He was waiting for me to give him my undivided attention before he spoke.

"What is it that you wish to talk to me about?" I asked quietly.

"My name is Franklin J. Beresford," he said as he looked at me.

I got the impression that he expected me to immediately know who he was and to be somewhat impressed by him. Needless to say, I wasn't impressed, surprised that he wanted to talk to me, but not impressed. It was clear that Mr. Beresford knew how thin the walls were in the house. When he spoke, he spoke quietly and slowly.

"That much I already know, Mr. Beresford. What is it you want?"

"I understand that you are a detective of some renown. I would like to hire you to find out what happened to Elizabeth Samuelson," he said without any change in his expression.

"It seems that there are a lot of people wanting to know what happened to her. What is she to you?"

"Can I trust you not to say anything to anyone else?" he asked, as he looked me straight in the eyes.

"Look, you're the one who came to me. It is obvious that you know a lot more about me then I know about you. If what you know about me is not to your liking, then I suggest that you find someone else to help you find out what happened to Elizabeth."

"You're quite right, Mr. McCord. I do know who you are," he conceded.

"So, would you mind getting to the point of this conversation?"

"Mr. McCord, Elizabeth Samuelson was my grand-mother."

Well, that came as a surprise. I immediately found myself interested in anything that he might have to say.

"My grandmother, the former Elizabeth Mae Beresford, married Bartholomew Samuelson. Elizabeth was an innocent girl of only eighteen at the time they were married. Bartholomew was much older and was already a ship's captain on a large sailing ship on the Great Lakes. He was often gone for weeks, sometimes for months at a time without coming home.

"Of course, Elizabeth would be left at home while he was out on the lakes. She would get very lonely. She did not have any family or friends in the area. Her entire family lived in the Chicago area.

"One summer while Bartholomew was out of port, she met a young man who was very poor. He did the gardening and other odd jobs around here. The young man fell in love with Elizabeth. He loved her very much, and she soon fell in love with him. They where able to carry on a relationship for almost two years before it came to a sudden end," he explained.

"Just how did it end?"

"I don't really know very much about that. All I know is that shortly after my father was born, Elizabeth and her lover suddenly disappeared, both at about the same time. There were a lot of rumors and speculations about what happened to them, but what actually happened to them is not known."

"What about your father? What happened to him?"

"One of the house maids took him to Elizabeth's parents in Chicago. They raised him as their own, giving him their last name. He is dead now," he said.

"I understand that you have been here since shortly after the body was found on the beach. Some people think the body was Elizabeth."

"That is correct. I have been here trying to find out if it was Elizabeth, and if it was what happened to her. If it was her, what was the cause of her death? She was so young to have died," he said, a note of sadness in his voice.

"Have you found out anything?" I asked in the hope that he might at least give me a clue.

"Regrettably, I have not. Have you been able to find out anything?"

"No, I'm afraid not. I have seen the police reports. There is nothing in them that would give any conclusive proof that the woman in the ice block was Elizabeth. I'm sorry," I said.

"I'm sorry, too. I think I should tell you that I know why you are here, Mr. McCord. You are here to find out who is trying to scare your friend away from this lodge. Please, let me assure you that I do not, and have not, had anything to do with that. My only interest is to find out what happened to my grandmother. I have no other interest in this place than that," he said as he stood up.

I had to wonder just how he knew why I was here, but then he was a smart man and probably had a lot of connections. Just the fact that he knew who I was would most likely have lead him to that conclusion.

"That's good to know," I said as I moved toward the door.

"If you find out anything that might be of help in my quest, I would appreciate whatever information you are able to provide. I would be more than happy to compensate you for your time and effort," he added.

I stepped over to the door and opened it. After making sure there was no one in the hall, I stepped back allowing him to leave my room.

As soon as he was gone, I stepped back into my room and closed the door. Needless to say, the information he had given me was interesting. I knew it would fit in with what I was trying to find out, sooner or later, but at the moment I wasn't sure how. I took a few moments to think over what he had said.

It seemed to me that every bit of information I was getting was leading me toward trying to solve the death of Elizabeth Samuelson. It was becoming clear that if I was to solve the problems that Tom was having, I was going to have to find out what happened to Elizabeth Samuelson, and her lover, first. There had to be some kind of a connection between the two, but at this point in time I couldn't see it.

CHAPTER SEVEN

I waited for a minute or so after Mr. Beresford left my room. I wanted Mr. Beresford to have a chance to leave without arousing any suspicion from anyone who might have seen him in the hall. By waiting until he had a chance to go downstairs or to his room, it gave me a couple of minutes to consider what Mr. Beresford had said.

As soon as I was sure that he was well on his way, I opened the door and checked the hall. There was no one around.

After locking the door to my room and making sure that it was secure, I started for the stairs. I stopped near the top of the stairs for a few seconds to look down on the main room.

The first thing I noticed was that Monica was sitting near the door, waiting for me. When she saw me, the worried look on her face seemed to melt away into a soft pleasant smile.

As I was coming down the stairs, I noticed Elinor Mortimer watching me over the top of the magazine she was pretending to read. I thought it was a little funny as she was reading the same magazine that she had been reading last night. I seriously doubted that she had found anything very interesting in that particular magazine, as it was a men's sports magazine and she just didn't strike me as the sports fan type.

Monica stood up as I came down the stairs and moved toward her. I had to admire her idea of what to wear when exploring old copper mines. The denim blouse she was wearing accented her firm full breasts and tapered down to a western style belt at her narrow waist. Her stretch jeans hugged the smooth curves of her body almost as if they had been made especially for her. Her narrow waist, the flare of her hips and her long legs made me almost forget that we were going out to find and explore old copper mines. I think if she had suggested returning to my room I would not have hesitated a single second to turn around and go back to my room.

"I was getting a little worried about you. What took you so long?" she asked in a whispered.

"I had a visitor," I replied softly.

"Who?" she asked, her expression turning more serious.

"I'll tell you about it later. This place has too many eyes and ears."

Monica took a quick look around to see if anyone was watching us. When she looked back at me, I smiled at her and the serious look on her face faded away.

"Elinor will just have to guess at what we're doing. Let's get out of here," I suggested.

Monica took my arm as I turned and led her toward the front door. We walked down the porch steps together. When we got to her car, I opened the door for her and she got in. After shutting the door, I went around to the other side of the car. As I was getting in, I looked up toward the west tower again. I saw a shadow on the curtain, but I could not make out if it was a man or a woman, or if it was just a shadow caused by light shining in from the other side of the tower. As I sat down and shut the door, Monica looked over at me.

"Did you see anyone?" she asked.

"No, just a shadow. Let's go, and drive away as if we are going back into town."

The puzzled look on Monica's face showed me that she was not sure what I was thinking. She reached for the key and started the car. Monica backed away from the lodge and then turned out onto the road. She headed in the direction of town.

"What's going on? Why are we taking the car if the mine is so close to the lodge?" she asked.

"If we started out walking up toward the ridge behind the lodge, whoever is watching us might be able to figure out right away what we are looking for. This way, they just might think we are going back into town for a little fun."

She responded with a slight nod as she ran the sports car through its gears. I watched in the side mirror to make sure that no one was following us and at the same time I watched for a place to turn off the highway.

"Turn here," I said as I pointed toward a narrow dirt road that appeared to wander back into the woods toward the shore.

As she slowed the car to turn, I looked both ways to make sure that no one would see us turn off the highway. I didn't see anyone in either direction as she turned onto the dirt road. As soon as we had gone far enough down the road to be out of sight of the highway, I had her stop the car while I kept watch behind us.

"Do you see anyone?" she asked.

I hesitated for a few moments before I answered her.

"No. I don't think we are being followed, and I don't think anyone saw us turn."

I turned around in the seat and faced toward the front of the car. My mind was trying to figure out who might have been in the tower. I could think of a lot of possibilities, but I had nothing to go on that would help me narrow it down to one particular individual.

"Now what do we do?" Monica asked.

Her question interrupted my thoughts and I looked over at her. She was looking at me and waiting for me to respond. I realized that I had other things to attend to now. I could worry about who was in the tower later.

I knew we would have to find a place to hide her car before we could try to find the mines. It would be better if we could find a place further from the main road and closer to the mine.

"I hope you have a good pair of hiking boots on, we have a long walk ahead of us."

"Do you know where the mine is from here?"

"It's over that way," I replied as I pointed back in the direction of the lodge. "I would guess it's about a mile from here."

"I take it we are walking from here?" Monica asked.

"No, I don't think so," I said as I looked at our surroundings. "I think we need to find a better place to hide the car first, and then we'll walk from there. Let's go down this road a little further and see if we can find a place to hide your car."

Monica smiled as she put the car in gear and began driving slowly along the road. I wondered what she found so amusing.

"You know you have a strange way of getting a girl alone with you out in the woods," Monica said with a hint of laughter in her voice.

"It works, doesn't it?" I asked with a grin.

She laughed softly as she reached over and put her hand on my leg. The sound of her soft laughter was pleasing to the ear. I had to admit that I could not have planned a day in the woods with a more beautiful woman if I had tried.

"Here. Pull in here," I said as I pointed to what looked more like a two lane cow path through the trees than it did a road.

Monica turned onto the narrow path that seemed to lead deeper into the woods. From the looks of it, it might have been an old mining road that hadn't been used for years. The old road was covered with weeds and low hanging branches from the trees as that grew over it. Monica glanced over at me several times as if she wanted to ask me if I was crazy.

We followed the old road for several hundred yards before we came to a place where small trees had grown up in the middle of the road. Monica stopped the car and looked at me. It looked as if this was as far as we were going to be able to go with the car.

We both looked around for a minute. It appeared that Mother Nature was slowly reclaiming the land. It was the perfect place to leave the car. For anyone to see it, they would have to be almost standing on it.

"This looks good," I said as I looked around. "No one will find it here."

"I just hope we can find it again," Monica said as she looked around while we got out of the car.

"We can find it," I assured her as I moved to the rear of the car.

I looked across the car at her and smiled. She smiled back and moved around to the rear of the car next to me. Monica took her key and opened the trunk. She got out two flashlights and handed one to me. We checked the flashlights to make sure that they worked before starting out.

"Say, you never did tell me who your visitor was," she said as she closed the trunk.

"My visitor was none other than Mr. Franklin J. Beresford."

"Really? I've heard of him. He's one of the riches men in Wisconsin. Was he the man sitting at the end of table?"

"Yes."

"What did he want from you?"

"He claims to be the grandson of Elizabeth Samuelson."

"You're kidding?" she asked with surprise.

"No. We best get going. I'll lead the way."

I started off in the direction that would lead us back toward where the old copper mine should be located. She followed closely behind me.

"That's it? He came to you to tell you who he was and that he was Elizabeth's grandson?"

"Well, no. Not actually."

"Well, tell me. Don't keep me in suspense," she said impatiently.

I told her about my brief conversation with Mr. Beresford as we worked our way through the woods. The more I thought about what he had said, the more interested I became in finding out if he was actually Elizabeth's grandson. I could see no reason that he would lie to me, but then nothing else was making any sense, either. What could he possibly gain by lying to me? There was also the fact that he had asked me to help him find out more about Elizabeth and her lover. Not once did he mention anything about Captain Samuelson.

"Do you really think that he is related to Elizabeth?"

"Yes," I replied, still not a hundred percent convinced of my answer.

"What makes you think so?"

Just as I was about to answer her question, I heard something off to my right. I stopped, reached out and took Monica by the hand. I pulled her down with me behind some bushes. As she knelt down next to me, we looked through the brush in the direction of the lake.

"What is it?" she asked in a whisper.

"Shhhhh."

I strained to listen. It sounded a bit like laughter. I motioned for Monica to follow me as I moved slowly through the woods toward the lake. When we reached the edge of the woods where we could see out onto the beach, we discovered a small cove. We knelt down behind a fallen tree. Not more than about fifteen feet down in front of us, on the sand, was a blanket, a picnic basket and a large white and orange beach umbrella.

We couldn't see anyone on the beach, but we could hear a girl giggling. It sounded as if the giggling was coming from further down the beach, somewhere behind a sand dune.

Suddenly, we saw a naked young woman come running out from behind a sand dune. She was being chased by a young man who was also naked. The young man caught up with her just as she got to the umbrella. The young man grabbed her, swung her around and took hold of her by the waist. He lifted her off her feet and held her to him as he carried her toward the blanket. Once they got to the blanket, they fell into each other's arms in the shade of the umbrella. The young woman quit laughing as she threw her arms around the neck of the man as he rolled her over onto her back and rolled up over her. Their lips met in a deep passionate kiss.

"That's the newlyweds from the lodge. I think we should let them have their privacy," I whispered as I turned toward Monica.

She looked at me, and then took another look at the naked couple on the beach. As she looked back me, she smiled.

"You're a romantic, a hopeless romantic," she whispered, as she grinned.

I turned and looked at her then said, "I just know that I would like my privacy if I were with you on the beach like them."

I didn't give her a chance to respond, but simply turned back and began moving slowly and quietly back into the woods away from the beach. I could sense that she was watching my every move as she followed me. I didn't think she knew quite how to take my last statement. For that matter, I wasn't sure what I meant either, it just sort of came out.

We continued to move through the woods in silence. I wasn't sure what was on her mind, but I was thinking of the two of us. I had to wonder what it would be like to spend an afternoon on the beach with her like the newlyweds. In fact, my mind was so consumed with thoughts of the two of us together on a deserted beach that I almost missed the entrance to what looked like an old copper mine. I stopped so suddenly, and Monica was so close behind me, that she ran into me.

"What is it?" she asked.

"Look," I answered as I pointed to what looked more like the entrance to a cave than to a mine.

"Is that what we're looking for?"

"I'm not sure if it's the right one, but it's definitely the entrance to a mine or a good size cave. You wait here. I'm going to try to get my bearings so I can tell if this is the mine we are looking for."

"Why don't we just check it out since we're here?" she suggested. "If we find what we're looking for, then we don't have to look any further. If we don't, we can continue to look. After all, we have all afternoon."

"Not only beautiful, but smart, too. I like that in a woman," I said as I gave her a wink.

She smiled at me as if to say thank you for the compliment. I didn't say anything more. I simply checked the flashlight to make sure it was still working. The opening to the mine was rather small and I had to bend down to enter the mine. Monica followed close behind me.

"Stay close. I don't want to lose you down here."

"Don't worry about that, I'm right behind you. Besides, you can't get rid of me that easily."

"I'm glad to hear that," I said jokingly.

We worked our way down into the mine. We had to go about fifty feet back in before the tunnel opened up into what looked like a fairly large room. The room was at least forty feet long and maybe twenty feet wide. The ceiling was at least ten to twelve feet high in most places. The floor appeared to be relatively smooth, but like the tunnel it slopped gently down and away from the mine entrance. It was much colder than I had expected since we were not very far from the entrance, and as far as I could tell we had not descended very deep. However, we were far enough from the entrance that we could not see any light from the outside.

As we stood at the entrance of the room, I shined the flashlight around slowly. About half way down the room and off to one side, I noticed several old wooden crates stacked almost to the ceiling. Other than those crates, the room appeared to be empty.

I also noticed a very dark area at the other end of the room. My first thought was that it was where the tunnel continued to go further down, possibly turning. I felt cold hands touch my arm and I turned to see Monica holding onto me.

"Are you okay?" I asked.

"Yes," she replied with a forced smile. "I'm just cold."

"I want to check out those crates and take a look down there, then we can get out of here," I said as I pointed the flashlight toward the darken area.

Monica followed me as we walked over toward the crates. We quickly discovered that there were two rows of crates and they all appeared to be very old. I also noticed that there were several crates that had been opened and discarded off to the side. On closer examination, we found them to be empty.

Shining the flashlight on the floor, I saw what appeared to be wheel tracks in the dirt. It looked as if there had been some crates wheeled across the floor on a two-wheel handcart. I could find no tracks indicating how the crates had gotten here in the first place. It was obvious that the crates had not recently been wheeled in here from the entrance that we had come through, but that some crates had been moved out of this room to somewhere else. The markings in the dirt indicated that there had been more crates here at one time, and not too long ago.

I followed the wheel tracks along the wall until they disappeared behind a very heavy oak plank door that was set in the rock wall.

"I wonder where that goes?" I asked myself in a whisper.

"I don't know, but I'm freezing."

I turned and looked at her. Monica was standing next to me with her arms across her chest and her hands moving up and down her arms trying to warm herself.

"Come on. Let's get out of here. We can come back and check out the rest of this later," I suggested.

She nodded her approval. I took hold of her hand and we went back through the tunnel to the entrance. As we approached the entrance and could see the light outside the mine, we could begin to feel the warmth of the day. Once we were outside in the sunshine, it didn't take long for us to warm up.

"That place is like a deepfreeze," Monica commented. "Did you notice that it got colder as we went further from the mine entrance?

She was right. It was very much like a very big deep-freeze. It was the perfect place to keep anything of almost any size frozen solid. It was the perfect place to keep a large block of ice frozen for years, even hundreds of years or more, I thought.

"I think we have found what we were looking for. I can't be sure, but I'd be willing to bet that this was where Elizabeth Samuelson was kept frozen in that block of ice for the past hundred years or so," I said, excited by what we had found.

But then I began to think. What did we find? All we saw were a number of large crates. We had no idea what was in them or where they had come from. Although there were indications that someone had been in the mine and had wheeled several of the boxes around, there was no way to know for sure just when that was or what was done with them. I was beginning to wish that I had spent more time in the mine, but it was cold in there and I was sure that we could come back again to examine the mine and its contents at a later time. The next time we would be better prepared for the cold temperatures inside the mine.

"We may have found where the block of ice was stored, but what I don't understand is how did she get into the block of ice in the first place?" Monica asked.

"I don't know for sure. This is just a theory mind you, but I think she was put in the mine to freeze to death.

"Why?"

"Why, I don't know yet. But anyway, she froze to death and was then put into the ice."

"What makes you think that?"

"The lab reports found no cause of death. If she froze to death in the mine and was then put in ice after she was dead, they wouldn't be able to find any cause of death except for freezing. If she drowned in the water and then it froze, there would have been evidence of her drowning."

"Who would do such a thing and why?" Monica asked.

"That I haven't figured out, but I have a pretty good idea where that door goes. I think it goes to the icehouse next to the lodge.

"If you're right, that would mean that Tom probably knows about this old mine. If he knows about the mine, then he knows more than he's telling you," Monica said almost apologetically.

I didn't want to believe what she was saying, but she did have a very good point. It was difficult for me to believe that Tom hadn't told me about this mine, unless he didn't know about it. At the same time, I found it hard to believe that he didn't know about the mine. He would have been over all the papers and the title and deed for the property before he bought it. The only way that he would not know about the mine was if it was not recorded as being on his land, but the mine being on the map indicated that it was registered and it was on his land.

"I hope you're wrong," I said as I mulled it over.

"I do, too," she said as if she were sorry that she had even mentioned it.

We started back through the woods toward the car. There were still a lot of unanswered questions, but I was convinced that we had found the place where Elizabeth had been kept frozen. I was also convinced that we had found something else, but just what I didn't know.

CHAPTER EIGHT

When we got back to Monica's car, we put the flashlights back in the trunk. We had warmed up by then and the cold of the mine was just a memory. I glanced at my watch and then looked at Monica.

"I think we're a little late for dinner at the lodge," I said.

"I'm sure you're right. What do you suggest we do for dinner?"

"How about going into Sturgeon Bay. I know we can find a nice place to eat there," I suggested.

"Okay," she agreed.

I thought that by driving into Sturgeon Bay for dinner it would give us a chance to talk and possibly share some of our thoughts about what was going on at the lodge. It would also give us a place to talk without the possibility of someone listening in on us.

Monica insisted that I drive. After she got into the car and I closed the door for her, I got behind the wheel and drove the little sports car back to the highway. I didn't want anyone to see us come out of the woods so I made sure that it was clear before pulling out onto the highway.

We cruised along the highway toward Sturgeon Bay with the top down and the breeze blowing in our hair. The sun was bright and felt good after the cold air inside the mine.

Monica reached over and rested her hand lightly on my leg. I glanced over at her and smiled. She smiled back at me and then tipped her head back against the headrest. When I glanced over at her again, she still had her head tipped back and her eyes closed. I wasn't sure if she had fallen asleep, or if she had just closed her eyes to help herself relax. I wondered if she was thinking, or if the very long day had made her tired enough to actually sleep. It had been a short night and a long day for both of us.

My own thoughts quickly returned to the mine. It was clear to me that the mine would be the almost perfect deepfreeze as it was cold and damp. Anything put in the mine would certainly freeze solid in a matter of a few hours and probably stay frozen for as long as it was there.

The mine had a rather small entrance. It required bending down and walking hunched over for some distance before it opened up into the large room. I was sure that contributed to the mine staying so cold even during the warm summer months. It was apparent that this mine was one that would hold the cold.

As my thoughts helped me envision the inside of the mine and what we had seen there, I began to think about where the tunnel at the far end of the room might lead. Did it just go deeper down into the mine, or did it go only a few feet further and stop? Was there a deeper mine shaft, or did it just turn the corner and end?

I also began to wonder about the door I discovered in the mine. It was a pretty heavy door. It was made of heavy oak planking with large carriage bolts holding them together. Did the door lead to the icehouse, or did it lead to some other place? My mind was filled with questions that only another trip into the mine could answer.

There was something about this mine that convinced me it was probably where Elizabeth had died, although I had nothing to go on except for the tracks of the two-wheel cart. I was already convinced that it was where she had been kept until someone took her out and placed her on the beach. But the big question that still remained unanswered was what did her death have to do with Tom's problem? Was she really a part of all this, or was she just a distraction?

I still couldn't understand why it was so important for me to find what and who caused Elizabeth's death? I couldn't figure out what it was that kept drawing me back to her. I couldn't seem to keep Tom's problems separated from Elizabeth's death. There had to be a connection between the two, but what was it?

My thoughts were interrupted when I felt Monica lightly squeeze my leg. I turned to glance at her.

"Thinking about the mine?" she asked with a smile.

"As a matter of fact, yes. We have to go back there. I think the mine holds a lot of clues, and possibly some answers."

"I agree," she said as she sat up straight. "I was thinking about it, too. I would like to know what's in all those crates."

"Yes, and where they came from. And where does the tunnel at the far end go?" I added.

"You said that Mr. Beresford claimed that Elizabeth was his grandmother, did he say who his grandfather was?"

"No, not really," I said giving it some more thought. "I can't put my finger on it, but I got the impression that he thinks his grandfather was probably Elizabeth's lover, and not Captain Samuelson. I'm not sure that Mr. Beresford really knows himself, but I think he is convinced that Elizabeth's lover was his grandfather. It's possible that is what he really wants to find out. The only thing he said for sure was that his father was raised by Elizabeth's parents in Chicago."

"I was wondering the same thing. If his real grandfather was Elizabeth's lover, not the captain, and Elizabeth's lover disappeared at or about the same time as she did, he might be frozen in ice somewhere, too," Monica suggested.

I took a moment to absorb what she was saying. Her deduction certainly had merit, enough merit to make it worth looking into. The only problem was where do I start looking.

"That's certainly a possibility. There's another thing that we might have overlooked," I said as I thought about the captain.

"What's that?"

"Whatever happened to Captain Samuelson?"

"You're right," she agreed. "We haven't given that much thought, either."

"I think we need to take a trip to the newspaper office for a look at some old newspapers," I suggested.

"Good idea. We can do that tomorrow. Right now, I would like to get something to eat, I'm starving," she said as she took hold of my arm, then leaned over and rested her head on my shoulder.

We didn't talk any more all the way into Sturgeon Bay. I enjoyed having her close to me as I drove. In fact, I enjoyed having her close to me anytime.

When we arrived in town, she looked around as we drove through the streets. We picked a restaurant that, by its appearance, had to be a lot nicer than the café where we had lunch. I parked the car in the parking lot and we went inside. A young woman met us at the door and showed us to a table in a secluded corner.

"A nice looking place," Monica commented as she sat down.

I looked around as I sat down. I had to agree with her. It was a whole world apart from the old café down the street. The place was more like a dinner club with small candles on each table and real linen tablecloths. Even the napkins were linen and neatly folded so that they stood up like little pyramids on the table. The glasses were sparkling in the candlelight and the silverware was placed perfectly on the table leaving room for the plates.

"A lot nicer then the café down the street. I just hope the food's good," I said with a grin.

The waitress walked up to the table and smiled politely.

"Would you like something to drink before dinner?" the waitress suggested.

"Sure," I replied, then looked to Monica for a response as to what she would like.

We ordered before-dinner drinks. They were followed by an excellent steak dinner with all the trimmings. After dinner, we ordered another drink and leaned back to relax for a little while. There was a small band over in the corner playing some slow, soft music that helped give the place a little extra touch of atmosphere. The small dance floor had only two or three couples dancing on it, moving easily to the music.

"Would you care to dance?" I asked.

"Yes," she replied with a smile.

I stood up, then pulled back Monica's chair as she stood up. Taking her hand in mine, I led her out onto the dance floor. I slipped my arm around her narrow waist and gently pulled her close to me.

As we moved to the slow rhythm of the music, she slid her hand up off my shoulder and around to the back of my head. She looked up into my eyes, but didn't say anything. The soft smile on her face and the sparkle in her eyes told me that she was happy and content being right where she was, in my arms.

Gently pulling her up against me, I could feel the warmth of her body and the firmness of her breasts as she pressed against me. She laid her head on my shoulder as I gently slid my hand down to the small of her back and held her tightly.

Suddenly, I noticed that the music had stopped. I wished that it would have continued, but the band was already leaving to take a short break. As I loosened my hold on her, she looked up at me and smiled. She took her hand from behind my neck, slid it down my arm and took hold of my hand. Together, we walked back to our table and sat down.

"Thank you, that was nice. I haven't danced for a long time," she said softly.

"You're welcome, but I should be the one thanking you."

She reached down and picked up her glass. She looked over the rim of the glass as she sipped the cool liquid from it. The sparkle in her eyes held my attention as I took a sip from my own glass.

"I think we should go back to the lodge pretty soon. I'm tired and we have a lot to do tomorrow," she suggested as she set her empty glass down on the table.

Reluctantly, I had to agree. It had been a long day and we still had the drive back to the lodge. As soon as I paid the check and placed a tip on the table, we left the restaurant. She again insisted that I drive. Once out on the highway, she again laid her head on my shoulder while I drove, but this time I didn't think about anything except the beautiful woman sleeping beside me.

When I pulled up in front of the lodge, I shut off the headlights of the car and then shut off the engine. Monica woke up and stretched as she looked around to see where she was.

"I guess I slept all the way back. I'm sorry."

"That's okay. I didn't mind at all. You ready to go inside?"

"Yes," she replied.

I started to reach for the door handle when I thought I noticed a movement out of the corner of my eye. I quickly looked toward the corner of the house. There was nothing there, but I was sure that I had seen something or someone move.

"What is it?" Monica asked in a whisper.

"I saw something move over by the corner of the lodge, but whatever it was seems to be gone now," I whispered.

I got out of the car and went around to the other side. I opened the door and reached out to help her out. Taking her hand, we walked up the short sidewalk and onto the porch. As I opened the door, I took another look toward the corner of the lodge before stepping inside. Again, I saw nothing. Whatever I thought I saw was gone.

Once inside, we noticed that the lights had been dimmed down for the night. There was no one in the main room at the late hour. We walked up the stairs and down the hall to Monica's room.

Stopping in front of her room, she took her key out of her pocket and unlocked the door. Turning around toward me, she reached up and put her hands on my shoulders.

"I enjoyed spending the day with you," she said softly as she looked up into my eyes.

"I had a good time, too."

As she gently pulled me toward her, I reached out and put my hands on her waist. I leaned down and kissed her lightly on the lips. Her lips were warm and soft. The last thing I wanted to do was to leave her.

Reluctantly, I pulled back and looked into her blue eyes. I wanted to invite her to come to my room to spend the night with me, but I didn't want to rush her into anything she might not be ready for, or might not want. Her eyes sparkled in the dim light of the hall. The look on her face gave me the impression that she was waiting for me to say something.

"Goodnight," I whispered.

"Goodnight," she replied with a soft sigh.

She gave me a quick peck on the cheek, then turned and disappeared into her room. As her door closed, I found myself wishing that I had asked her to spend the night with me. I was missing her already.

After I heard her lock the door, I turned and went into my room. When I first entered my room, I didn't notice anything out of the ordinary. I guess my mind was too occupied with thoughts of Monica. It took a few moments for it to register in my mind that the adjoining door on my side was open. I thought I had closed it before we left, but I wasn't a hundred percent sure. Since it was already open, I decided to leave it open for now. I guess deep down I was hoping that Monica would decide to come to my room later.

I went into the bathroom and took a quick shower, then crawled into bed. I shut off the bedside lamp. As I lay on my bed with my hands behind my head looking up at the ceiling, my mind sort of ran over the events of the day. With so many things running through my mind, I found it hard to fall asleep. It was then that I realized that it was quiet, too quiet.

From the very first day here in the lodge, I had heard all kinds of little sounds. Sounds like the wind, the rain, the subtle creaking that is so typical of old houses like this one, water running in other parts of the house and other sounds that could not be so easily identified.

Then it hit me, I had not heard even a hint of a sound from Monica's room. I was sure she would have taken a shower, or at least washed her face. I should have heard running water, but I hadn't heard anything.

I began to worry about her. Had she decided to simply go to bed without a shower? That didn't seem like her. After all, we had spent some time in the woods and in a mine. She certainly would have wanted a shower after that.

My imagination was starting to get the best of me. I couldn't help but wonder if someone had been in her room when she came in? That was possible, but who and for what reason?

The more I thought about it, the more worried I became. I was beginning to think that the lodge was beginning to affect my mind. I didn't want to look like a fool by barging in on her, but I would never forgive myself if I didn't check to see if she was all right. I decided that I would go with my gut feeling.

I reached over and turned on the bedside lamp, then got out of bed. I quickly slipped into a pair of slacks. As I reached for the doorknob of the adjoining door to her room, I hesitated. I had to wonder if I was being foolish and what she would think when I came barging into her room. I didn't want to disturb her if she was asleep, but something inside kept nagging at me to check on her, and do it now.

When I turned the knob, I discovered that her adjoining door was unlocked. I opened the door and looked in. The light from my room lit up only a small part of her room. I could see her bed, but she was not in it. My heart skipped a beat and then began to pound as I wondered where she could be.

I stepped into her room for a quick look around. It was then that I heard a soft, almost inaudible moan, coming from the other side of her bed. I quickly moved around the foot of the bed to the other side where I found Monica lying on the floor.

I knelt down on the floor beside her and lifted her into my arms. She seemed very groggy as if she had been knocked out. As she started to come around, she looked up at me with blank and wondering eyes.

"What happened?" she asked.

"I don't know. I was about to ask you the same thing."

"Someone was in my room. I remember locking the door. Just as I went to turn on the light, someone grabbed me from behind and put a cloth over my mouth. That's the last thing I remember," she said softly.

"Come on, you're going to stay with me tonight. Can you get up?"

"Yes, I think so," she replied weakly.

I helped her to her feet and then carefully guided her into my room. She sat down on the edge of my bed and took several deep breaths. Her head cleared quickly from the effects of whatever it was that was used to knock her out.

"You're staying here," I insisted.

"I can't stay in these clothes. I need a shower."

"Are you sure?" I asked, concerned that the effects of the drugging had not fully worn off.

"I'm okay," she replied smiling at me.

"I'll get you what you need. You can take a shower in my bathroom. Can you stand up okay?" I asked.

I watched her as she stood up next to the bed. She seemed to have recovered without any side effects, but I was still worried about her.

"You okay?"

"Yes, I'm fine now," she insisted as she walked toward the bathroom. "I feel fine. A shower will do me good."

"What do you want me to get for you to wear?" I asked as I watched her walk toward the bathroom.

She stopped at the bathroom door, slowly turned and looked back toward me. A soft smile came over her face. I was sure that she was trying to relieve my worries.

"Would a towel be too much?" she asked in that same soft and sexy voice I had heard the first time I met her.

I smiled and replied in a whisper, "No."

She gave me a wink, then turned and disappeared into the bathroom.

I was still a little worried about her, but whatever had been used to knock her out hadn't lasted very long and apparently didn't have any side effects. My thoughts quickly returned to where I found her in her room. It didn't take a genius to figure out that this place was no longer safe for her.

I went into her room and turned on a light. Someone had gotten into her room. There had to be some kind of a clue as to who and for what reason. The first thing I checked was the latch on her door. It did not look like it had been forced. The fact that it had not been forced made me wonder if whoever had been in her room had a key. Since the doors between our rooms had been unlocked, there was the possibility that whoever it was had come in through my room.

After checking my door and finding that it had not been forced either, it began to look as if someone either had a key to at least one of the rooms, or was very handy with a set of lock picks.

I looked around the rest of the room, but discovered nothing that would give any indication as to how they got into her room, or what they wanted. I wondered what they had been looking for, and if they found it. My first thought was the police report that Monica had shown me, but after giving it some thought I could think of nothing in it that would mean anything to anyone else.

As I stood in my room thinking about what had happened, I heard the shower stop running. I locked the door between our rooms and made sure that it was secure. I turned off the lights, slipped out of my slacks and crawled back into bed. Within a few minutes, Monica opened the door and stood in the doorway to the bathroom. The light behind her silhouetted her for just a few seconds before she shut the light off.

I watched her as he slowly walked toward my bed. She appeared as just a shadow in the dim light that came in through the window as she moved across the room. When she got close, I lifted the sheet inviting her to join me in the bed.

She was beautiful, and I couldn't take my eyes off her as she stood beside the bed wearing just a towel. She reached up, slowly unwrapped the towel and let it slide down the smooth lines of her body onto the floor at her feet.

She slid into bed beside me with the grace of a woman with class. I pulled the sheet up over her as she rolled up against me. Her naked body felt warm against my skin.

I wrapped my arms around her and held her close to me. She laid her head on my shoulder as she snuggled up against me. Laying her arm across my chest and curling one of her shapely long legs over my legs, she moaned softly as I gently stroked her back with my hand. She yawned and then seemed to relax.

I laid there with her and listened to her breath. Her skin was like silk under my hand and her hair brushed lightly on my chest like a feather.

It didn't take very long before she was fast asleep. It was clear that she felt safe and secure with me, and that gave me a feeling of contentment. I had to admit that I felt very comfortable with her warm, naked body curled up against me.

We were both very tired and we needed a good night's sleep. It was enough for me to just have her close for now. She moved very slightly when I yawned. I felt very relaxed and at peace. It did not take me long to follow her lead and fall into a deep restful sleep.

CHAPTER NINE

For the first several hours of the night, I found myself waking up fairly often to check on Monica. After what had happened, I needed to know that she was safe and that everything was all right. It was pretty late before I finally was able to get some good solid sleep.

When I finally did wake up, it was to the feel of a soft, warm hand moving slowly over my chest. Her fingers running through the hair on my chest as she laid quietly behind me. The feel of a warm naked body tucked up against my back gave me a feeling of contentment. Monica's breath was like a soft gentle breeze against the back of my neck as she snuggled up against me.

I slowly reached back and put my hand on the soft skin of her hip. I gently stroked her hip and thigh as I enjoyed the feel of her hand on me. She moaned softly and wrapped her arms around me, squeezing me tightly.

"You feel good," she whispered and then she kissed the back of my neck.

"So do you," I replied softly.

As I started to move, Monica unwrapped her arms from around me so that I could roll over on my back. I rolled over and looked into her cobalt blue eyes that sparkled in the morning light that crept into the room from around the edges of the drapes that hung over the long narrow windows. She smiled as she leaned toward me until our lips met. As we kissed, she moved up over me, stretching her sexy body over me. Her firm breasts pressed against my chest as she pressed her lips against mine.

When the kiss was over, she lifted her head a little and smiled down at me. She lowered her head as she wrapped her arms around my neck and we once again kissed passionately.

I slid my hands from her sides up onto her back. She murmured softly as I slid my hands up and down the gentle contours of her back, from her neck to her shapely behind. Her skin was smooth and soft, yet her body was firm and exciting. The feel of her body as I ran my hands off her shoulders, down to the small of her back, up over her firm behind was unbelievable. That, along with the slow movement of her body over me as we kissed, and her firm breasts pressing against my chest was almost more than any man could endure. It was certainly more than this man could endure.

She raised herself up again and propped her chin up on her hands as she looked down at me. We were both breathing pretty hard. The passion of the moment showed in her eyes.

"I think we are going to miss breakfast again," she whispered as she looked at me with a devilish grin.

"Not if we hurry," I replied.

"Ooooh, but I don't want to hurry," she said in a soft, sexy voice.

"Me, either," I agreed, almost unable to say anything.

I slid my hands up her body to the back of her neck and gently pulled her face back down to mine. As our lips met, I tucked my arms along her sides. As we continued to kiss, I gently rolled her over onto her back. I slid one hand up over one of her breasts. Her breast was soft, yet firm, and it felt good in my hand. She moaned softly as I gently slid the palm of my hand over her hard nipple.

"That feels good," she murmured softly.

I rose up a little and looked down at her. Her golden hair was fanned out over the pillow. It framed her lovely face making her the most beautiful woman I had ever seen.

The look in her eyes told me that she liked the way I touched her, and I liked touching her.

"You are beautiful," I whispered.

A soft warm smile came over her face as she put her hand over mine. She held my hand firmly against her breast and looked into my eyes. Her eyes had a dreamy look to them.

"I wouldn't mind spending a day on the beach with you like the newlyweds," she said in a soft whisper.

I smiled. "I'd like that, too."

Just as I was about to lean down and kiss her again, we heard the door to the room next to mine slam shut. The loud sound of the door slamming startled both of us. We looked at each other as we wondered what was going on in the next room.

The suddenness of the interruption seemed to bring my attention back to the real reason that I was there. Rising up on my elbows, I reluctantly rolled away from Monica and sat up on the edge of the bed to listen.

"Well, I see you're up," a female voice said sarcastically.

"Damn you, I didn't plan on anything like this. Was it entirely necessary?" a voice asked angrily.

"Yes, and keep your damn mouth shut. You want everyone to hear you?"

The second voice sounded like a man. I glanced back at Monica and she looked at me. We had no idea what they were talking about, but we listened in an effort to find out.

"Everyone's gone, or is downstairs," the man insisted.

There was a pause before we heard the woman's voice again. Only this time it was almost too quiet to hear.

"I'm not so sure. Have you seen that young woman or that McCord fellow?" the woman's voice asked.

Monica sat up and knelt behind me on the bed, putting her hands on my shoulders as she leaned up against my back.

We tried to listen for any kind of clue as to what they were talking about, but they had toned down their conversation so much that we couldn't understand any more of what was being said. All we could hear was some faint mumbling.

It was apparent that one of them had done something that the other didn't approve of, or had not planned on, but what? From the conversation, I got the impression that it was something that one of them thought was pretty serious, but I had no idea what it could be.

"Did you recognize either of the voices?" Monica asked in a whisper.

"No, not for sure. I think the woman might be Elinor Mortimer."

"Could be, but I'm not sure," Monica said thoughtfully. "I wonder what she is doing in Andrew Thorndike's room?"

"I don't know," I replied as I thought about what was said.

I still had no idea what was going on, but I had a gut feeling that whatever it was it had to do with Tom. I still had nothing solid to base my feelings on.

I turned my head and looked over my shoulder at Monica. It didn't take but a second of looking at her for me to turn my thoughts back to her.

Here I was in a comfortable bed with one of the most beautiful women in the world, who just happened to be wearing nothing at all, and my mind was off in another world trying to figure out what was going on in the next room. I must be crazy, I thought.

Monica must have sensed what was on my mind. The smile on her face slowly faded as she looked at me. I got the impression that she must have remembered why she was here, too.

"I think we better get dressed. We have a lot to do before we can spend a day on a quiet little beach away from the rest of the world," she whispered in my ear.

It was not what I wanted to hear, but I knew she was right. Neither one of us was here for fun. She was here to get information on the lodge before it was a lodge. I was here to help my friend and to learn more about the history of the lodge.

She leaned over my shoulder and kissed me lightly then turned around and slid off the bed. I found it impossible to take my eyes off the smooth flowing lines of her naked body as she walked away from me and went toward the door to her room.

Just before she stepped out of sight, she glanced back over her shoulder, smiled and whispered, "Fifteen minutes," then winked at me.

I smiled at her and gave her a wink before she disappeared into her room, closing the door behind her. As soon as she was gone, I got up and went into the bathroom. I was dressed and ready to go back into the mine by the time she returned to my room.

She was wearing a pair of dark blue slacks and a flowered blouse. In her hand, she carried a rather heavy sweater. It didn't take much for me to figure out that she was ready to go back into the mine. Only this time, she was going a little better prepared for the cold.

"I don't think it's a good idea for us to carry sweaters and jackets so everyone can see them when it's shorts and short sleeves weather. Let's put them in this," I said as I opened a small tote bag.

She handed me her sweater and I put it in the bag along with my jacket. I took a quick look around the room to make sure everything was where it belonged. Before we left the room, I went into her room to make sure that her room was locked from the inside. I had no desire to expose her to another attack like last night.

As we left my room and I turned to lock the door, Elinor Mortimer and Andrew Thorndike come out of the room next to mine. It was apparent by the look on their faces that they hadn't expected to run into anyone in the hall at this hour.

Seeing them come out into the hall seemed to fluster Andrew a little, but for just a second or two. He quickly recovered. Although Andrew didn't say a word, it was clear that he was upset about something, and I doubted that it was because they ran into us.

He glared at us with the cold and harsh look of a man who was not afraid to do whatever he thought was necessary to accomplish his goals. He looked as if he wanted to say something really nasty or sarcastic, but apparently thought better of it. Instead, he quickly turned away and hurried off down the hall to the stairs. It seemed to me that he could not get away from us fast enough. That made me wonder what was going on between the two of them.

Elinor, however, reacted much differently. She recovered from her surprise at seeing us very quickly and even smiled at us. I suppose you could call that chilling stare along with lips that just slightly turned up at the ends to form something that could be mistaken for a smile.

The expression on her face may have had the appearance of a smile, but there was no smile in those hard, cold eyes of hers. At that very moment, I couldn't remember ever seeing eyes that were so intense and dangerous looking. The look in her eyes sent a chill down the back of my neck. It was clear to me that she had not wanted to be confronted by anyone, especially us.

I had to admire Monica's cool in responding to Elinor's glaring look at us. She simply smiled pleasantly and said, "Good morning. Isn't it a lovely day to go to the beach?"

Elinor quickly glanced at the bag Monica was holding and replied, "Why, yes, my dear. It is a very nice day to go to the beach."

Elinor's voice was sweet. In fact, so sweet that it almost made a person sick. I was glad that she didn't want to stay around and talk. She turned and walked briskly toward the stairs. As she turned the corner to go down the stairs, she glanced back at us. The phony smile was gone, but the hard, cold, penetrating look in her eyes was still there. I got the feeling that she might be afraid that we had heard her conversation with Andrew.

"I don't think that woman is very happy. I get the feeling that she didn't want us to see her with Mr. Thorndike," Monica said as she took hold of my arm.

"You're probably right. I'd be very careful around her. Don't turn your back on her or Thorndike, for that matter."

"I wonder what those two have in common. There's something about them that keeps bugging me, but I just can't put my finger on it," I said more to hear myself think than to really ask a question.

"What are you talking about, Nick?"

"Nothing," I replied with a smile. "I was just thinking out loud. We should get going."

Monica let go of my arm and I took her by the hand as we started down the hall. As we turned and started down the stairs, I made it a point of looking over the main room to see who might be around at this time of day.

Mr. and Mrs. Mortimer were sitting at a small table in one corner of the room. Mrs. Mortimer was trying very hard not to let us know that she was watching us. She was so obvious about it that her effort was almost laughable.

Mr. Mortimer glanced up at us, and then quickly looked down at the floor in front of him. He didn't seem the least bit interested in watching us. In fact, he seemed not to want to be seen at all.

I noticed that Mr. Thorndike was sitting near a small writing desk. He appeared to be writing a letter, or something, and did not seem to be interested in anything else. I took a quick look around the room for his wife, but didn't see her. I couldn't explain it, but for some reason it struck me as strange that she was not there. I had never seen him without her.

Monica and I didn't stop in the main room, but went directly out the front door to her car. As we got in the car, we automatically looked up toward the tower, but we saw nothing this morning.

"I don't think anyone is up there now," I said as I reached down to start the car.

"I didn't see anyone, either," Monica confirmed.

I started the car and backed out of the parking space. As we pulled away from the lodge, I looked in the rearview mirror and saw Elinor step out the door onto the porch and watch us leave.

"Elinor seems to be very interested in us this morning," I said as I pulled out onto the road toward town.

"Do you think she will follow us?"

I glanced in the rearview mirror and saw no one behind us before I answered.

"I don't think so, but it sure won't hurt to keep our eyes open to make sure."

I took a quick second look behind as I slowed down to make the turn onto the dirt road that wandered back into the woods. I stopped as soon as we were out of sight of the highway and watched to see if we were being followed. As soon as I was sure that it was safe, I drove the car to the same place we had parked it the day before. We took our bag from the trunk and the flashlights. Leaving the car, we walked through the woods toward the mine.

When we arrived at the mine, the sun was shining through the trees casting shadows on the ground making it almost impossible to see the entrance to the mine. I took a look around to make sure that no one else was near. I had a feeling we were not very far from the lodge, maybe a few hundred feet.

"The lodge should be over that way," I whispered as I pointed toward the southeast.

"Are you sure?"

"No, but one way to find out is to go look."

I slowly began working my way through the woods in the direction that would take us toward the lodge. Monica followed along behind. Just as I was about to step around a small tree, I noticed what looked like an opening in a small outcropping of rock. The opening was partially hidden by a berry bush. I decided that it might be a good idea to find out what was behind the bush.

As I pushed the bush aside, I realized that I had discovered an opening to another mine, or possibly a cave. I glanced back at Monica and reached out a hand.

"I think we should check this out," I whispered.

She nodded as she reached in the bag and got a flashlight out. She handed it to me and then waited for me to check out the entrance.

The entrance was rather small and I had to bend down in order to see in. I quickly discovered that it was not a mine at all, but a cave that went back about twenty feet or so, and the floor of the cave dropped rather steeply to a relatively flat area about the size of a small room. However, the room was large enough to stand up in.

"It's just a small cave. Nothing in it," I said quietly as I backed out, stood up and shut off the flashlight.

We moved around the bushes and continued working our way toward the lodge. As we came to the edge of woods and I could see out into the open, I grabbed Monica by the arm and pulled her down behind some bushes and a tree with me. There in front of us was the lodge.

We were behind the lodge. From where we were hidden, we could see all of the back and the west end of the lodge. We could also see the back of one of the towers, the one that we had seen movement in earlier. We saw no movement in the tower.

We ducked down even lower when we heard the back screen door open. One of the cooks, a rather large, heavyset man, stepped out the back door. He had a large pan in his hands that was filled with ears of corn. We watched him as he sat down on the step and began to tear the husks off the ears of corn.

"Looks like we will be having corn on the cob with dinner tonight," Monica whispered.

"Sure does," I replied as I looked around the area.

"You see that mound over there?" I asked as I pointed to a slight rise in the lawn about thirty or forty feet from the back of the house.

Monica looked in the direction I was pointing.

"Yes," she replied.

"My guess is that's the icehouse."

"What makes you think so? I don't see any way in."

"Remember what the lady at the courthouse said? She said that some of the larger houses owned by the rich had icehouses that were connected to the house by short tunnels."

"You might be right," she said thoughtfully.

"I think there's also a tunnel from the icehouse to the mine."

Monica looked at me with a gleam in her eye and smiled.

"The heavy oak door. You think it leads to the icehouse?"

"I sure do, and I think it's time to find out."

We carefully backed away and moved back deeper into the woods. When we were a safe distance from the lodge and we were sure that we could not be seen, we straightened up and walked back to the mine entrance.

CHAPTER TEN

When Monica and I got back to the mine, I set the tote bag down on a log near the entrance. I opened the bag, removed Monica's sweater and gave it to her. While she slipped into her sweater, I put my jacket on. I then checked the flashlights again. If the flashlights failed while we were in the mine, we could find it very difficult to find our way out in the dark.

Taking Monica by the hand, I squeezed her hand gently before we entered the mine. We worked our way through the tunnel until we were once again in the large room inside the mine. I stopped and shined my flashlight around the room in an effort to reacquaint myself with where things were and where we were in relation to the entrance, and to see if anything might have changed since yesterday.

"Take a look over there," I whispered as I shined my flashlight toward the stacks of crates.

Monica directed her flashlight toward the crates and looked at the crates.

"I don't see anything, just the crates."

"When we were here yesterday there were more crates. The first row was three crates high, now it's only two high. Someone has been in here since we were here."

"You're right. And one of the crates is missing. I wonder what happened to it."

"I don't know," I replied as I continued to look around.

I moved closer to the crates and shined the flashlight on the dirt floor near the base of the crates. Sure enough, there were several sets of wheel tracks in the dirt. From what I could tell, they looked like the tracks of a two-wheeled handcart, the same two-wheeled handcart we had seen tracks from yesterday.

As I examined the wheel tracks, I noticed two, possibly three sets of tracks went in one direction, while only one set went in a different direction. There was also a set of tracks that apparently came from where the handcart had been stored near the wall.

A single set of tracks seemed to go from the stack of crates to down deeper into the mine and back. The other sets of tracks seemed to go around behind the stack of crates toward the oak door.

"Someone moved one of the crates. Where do you think they took it?" she whispered.

"I don't know, but we're going to try to find out. I'm not sure, but I think more than one crate has been moved out of here. My guess would be that at least two, possibly three crates have been removed."

"Where were they taken?" Monica asked.

"I think at least two, maybe three, were taken out of here through that door. One was taken somewhere else, somewhere down there," I said as I pointed my flashlight toward the far end of the room.

I picked out the set of tracks that seemed to go toward the far end of the room. The tire tracks of the cart appeared to be just a little wider and left clearly defined marks in the dirt on the floor of the mine. From the look of the tracks, it was my guess that the cart had had a lot of weight on it when it was moved.

I decided to follow the clearer tracks to see where they went. As I began following the tracks across the room, Monica reached out and took hold of my arm. I got the feeling that she had no desire to let me leave her there while I checked out the lower end of the room.

The wheel tracks led down the slightly sloped floor away from the door and away from the entrance to the mine.

When we got to the end of the room, we quickly discovered that there was a tunnel that led off to the left and continued to go down deeper underground.

We also discovered a crate setting just a few feet inside the tunnel. Whoever had moved the crate had set it down right in the middle of the tunnel, almost blocking it off.

"Well, I guess that answers the question of where this crate went," I whispered.

Monica looked at the crate, and then looked down into the dark tunnel.

"It sure does, but where does the tunnel go and why was the crate moved from the stack to here?"

"I don't know," I replied as I started to squeeze my way around the crate.

There was just enough room in the tunnel for us to get by the crate if we moved up against the wall. As I slid past the crate, I shined the flashlight down the tunnel in an effort to see how far it went, but I couldn't see the end of it.

After going a little farther down the tunnel, it looked as if the tunnel came to an end in about another fifteen feet or so. Monica followed me until we came close to the end. At the end of the tunnel, we found that it dropped down about six to eight feet. Shining my flashlight down into the hole, I could see nothing but ice.

I took several minutes to look down into the hole and study the ice. It didn't look like fresh ice to me. It appeared to be somewhat opaque, sort of frosted and yellowed with age, but then I'm no expert on ice. The hole looked like it might be an old mineshaft that had probably filled with water when mining was discontinued then froze. The one thing I was sure of was that it had been full of ice for many years, and there would be no way of telling how deep down the ice in the shaft went without drilling down into it.

Then I noticed something in the light that at first seemed strange. It looked to me as if a rather large section of the ice might have been either cut or chipped out and removed, but I couldn't be sure. It seemed strange that someone would be coming in here to get ice. I couldn't think of one practical use for such old, dirty and most likely stale ice.

"Take a look here," I said as I pointed my light down into the shaft.

Monica moved up beside me and looked down into the shaft. With the addition of her flashlight shining into the shaft, it became clear that a rather large piece of ice had been cut out and removed.

I began to wonder if this was the place where Elizabeth's body had been for the past hundred years or so. The more I thought about it, the more convinced I became that it was. The area where the ice had been removed would have been large enough to contain a body.

"I think we may have found where Elizabeth had been resting for over a hundred years."

"You mean here, in the ice?" Monica asked, her expression indicating that she wasn't as sure as I was.

"Yes. If you look carefully, you can see what looks to be a hole in the ice down there. It looks as if someone has cut out a large block of the ice. It looks to me to be large enough that it could have easily contained Elizabeth's body."

Monica continued to look down at the ice as if she was studying it. I had no idea what she was thinking, but if she was thinking along the same lines I was she was wondering how they got the ice out of there.

"How in the world would they have gotten a block of ice that big out of here?" she asked.

"That's a good question and I don't have a good answer," I replied as I began looking around for an answer.

As I shined my flashlight around, I noticed a pile of heavy ropes and several large pulleys stacked back in a dark corner. I shined my flashlight up on the ceiling and saw a large hook with a heavy pulley hooked to it directly above the hole.

"There's your answer," I said as I pointed my flashlight up toward the ceiling.

"This place gives me the willies. It's like being in somebody's tomb," Monica whispered as she squeezed my arm.

"I think it was somebody's tomb, Elizabeth's tomb."

"Can we get out of here?"

"Sure."

Monica turned around and was ready to leave while I stopped to take one last look down into the mineshaft. Just as I was about to turn around to join her, her flashlight shined on the back of the crate that had been left in the tunnel.

"Oh, God!" Monica gasped as she put a hand over her mouth and turned her flashlight away from the crate.

I quickly turned toward Monica to see what had startled her. I shined my flashlight at the crate. There was a small hand hanging out the back of the crate. It appeared to be a woman's hand.

As I walked past Monica toward the crate, she grabbed hold of my arm and followed very close behind, peering over my shoulder. She stepped back a step as I bent down and reached out to the crate. I took hold of the back of the crate and pulled hard on it. The crate popped opened and a body sorted of rolled part way out. Needless to say, I was surprised to find the frozen body of a woman stuffed inside the crate.

"Oh, my God! It's Mrs. Thorndike," Monica uttered, then quickly turned away.

It was Mrs. Thorndike, all right. She had been neatly stuffed into the crate. Her skin was covered with frost and her eyes were open, but they were not seeing anything. She was dead. She was wearing only a thin nightgown, which led me to believe that she had been murdered sometime last night then taken to the mine and put in the crate.

I bent down to take a closer look at her. The bruise marks on her neck indicated that someone who was very strong had strangled her. By the way her head was hanging off to one side, I was sure that her neck had been broken as well.

As I turned to comment on the cause of death to Monica, I noticed that she had her back to me. It was clear that finding Mrs. Thorndike like this had upset her.

I stood up and went to her. I took her in my arms and held her tightly in an effort to comfort her. Monica turned around in my arms and held onto me as she buried her face in my shoulder so that she would not have to look at the body.

As soon as she regained her composure enough to walk, I led her around the crate and back into the main part of the mine. We started toward the entrance to the mine. When we got to the other crates, I stopped.

"There's one thing that I need to check out before we leave. Wait here?" I said as I guided her away from the crate toward the entrance to the mine.

"I want to get out of here, please," she pleaded.

"I'll be just one minute. I promise. I have to check out that door."

It was clear that seeing Mrs. Thorndike like that had shaken her, but I had to confirm my suspicions. I handed her the flashlight. There was enough light that I could see the large plank door from where we stood.

"Stay here and shine the light toward the door. I'll only be a minute and I won't be out of your sight."

I let go of her and quickly moved across the room toward the heavy oak door. The first thing I noticed was that there was no lock on this side of the door. I tried the door, but it wouldn't open. It was clear that it was locked from the other side. I also noticed that the wheel tracks went under the door, which reaffirmed my suspicions that the crates were being taken through the door.

"Nick, please!" Monica begged.

I quickly returned to Monica and took the flashlight from her. She took hold of my arm and we hurried out of the mine into the clean fresh air.

Monica let out a heavy sigh of relief and sat down on the log where we had left our tote bag. She shivered even though she still had her sweater on and it was warm outside of the mine. I sat beside her and wrapped her in my arms in an effort to calm her and comfort her. She leaned against me as she gradually regained her composure.

"I'm sorry," she whispered.

"It's okay," I assured her.

"I'm not used to seeing dead people like that," she said as she looked at me, pleading for me to understand.

"I'm sure you're not."

"Who would want to kill Mrs. Thorndike?" she asked, her eyes pleading for an answer.

"I don't know."

I was wondering the same thing, except that the more I thought about it the more I wonder who Mrs. Thorndike really was. Was she related to the Samuelsons or the Mortimers in some way, or was she just someone who knew too much and become too much of a liability?

I stood up, took off my jacket and put it in the tote bag. Monica had regained her composure and took off her sweater. I put it in the tote bag with my jacket.

I looked around to see if there were any tracks around the entrance to the mine. I wanted to be sure that no one would know that someone had been in there. With the rocky ground near the entrance, it was impossible to see any signs of tracks at all. I took a few steps away from the log in the direction of the lodge, and then stopped to look through the woods.

"What is it?" Monica asked.

I turned back toward her and could see the puzzled look on her face. I stepped up in front of her and took her by the arm.

"I think we better get out of here," I said as I helped her to her feet.

Monica didn't resist one bit. She was as ready to get away from the mine as I was. I grabbed up the tote bag and we hurried back toward her car.

By the time we arrived at the car we were both out of breath. I pitched the tote bag in behind the seat and then opened the door for her. As soon as she was in the car, I got in. As I reached down to turn the key and start the car, I suddenly realized something that I had overlooked.

"What's the matter?" she asked.

It was obvious that she didn't understand why I hesitated to start the car. I was sure that she was ready to get away from here as fast as possible.

I wasn't even sure that what suddenly hit me was what really happened. I had nothing to base my thoughts on except for a long time as an investigator.

"I'll bet Elizabeth's lover is buried in that ice," I said more to hear my thoughts out loud than to provide an answer to Monica's question.

"What?"

"When I talked to Mr. Beresford, he said that his grandmother, Elizabeth, and her lover disappeared at about the same time. If Elizabeth Samuelson was frozen in the ice in that mine, then I think there's a very strong possibility that her lover is buried in the ice, too."

"We have to go to the police," she said.

"Did you see Mr. Thorndike in the main room this morning?"

"Yes. So did you. What about it?" Monica said, her response indicating that she had no idea what I was thinking.

"Do you remember what he was doing?"

"Writing, I think," she answered, as she began to wonder what I was getting at.

"That's right. He sure didn't look like a man who had just lost his loving and devoted wife, did he?"

"He may have thought that she was still in their room," she suggested.

"But he had just come out of his room with Mrs. Mortimer. He had to know that she was not there."

"You're right," she said with surprise. "I'll bet that's what they were talking about. He already knew that she was dead."

"He not only knew it, but I think he was directly involved in killing her," I said as the pieces of the puzzle seemed to begin to fall into place.

"What makes you think that? We heard him say that he didn't plan on it," she reminded me.

"It may not have been in their plans, but I'd be willing to bet that was there and that he helped move her to the mine."

"What kind of man would kill his own wife, or stand by and let her be killed?"

"Possibly the kind that wasn't really her husband," I suggested.

"I don't get it," she replied.

"Did you ever see him show her the slightest bit of affection?"

Monica thought for a second or two then said, "No, not that I recall."

"And this morning, he showed no sign that he even missed her. In all the times that we saw them together, I never saw him show the least bit of attention to her. I don't remember ever seeing them even speak to each other."

"That's true, but a lot of men don't speak to their wives," Monica said.

"True, but the way he looked at her is not the way a man looks at his wife."

"Why would they pretend to be married?"

"That I can't answer."

"We need to tell the police," she stated again.

"You're right, of course."

I started the car and drove back to the highway. Before turning out onto the highway, I checked both ways to see if anyone might be around. It was clear, so I turned out onto the highway and headed toward Sturgeon Bay.

There seemed to be a lot of pieces of this puzzle that didn't fit together. I spent most of the driving time thinking about each one of the guests at the lodge. I immediately eliminated the newlyweds as being involved in anything except themselves.

Mr. Beresford didn't seem to be a likely candidate as the murderer. He had too much to risk, was a loner, and was hardly big enough to have moved Mrs. Thorndike's body from the lodge to the mine by himself. He just didn't seem to fit the profile of a killer. If he was the killer, he would have to have had help from someone else. His help may have come from a couple of very loyal employees who got paid very well to help him, but I doubted that he was the kind to get others involved with anyone who might not keep their mouths shut. He wouldn't open himself up to blackmail.

Now, on the other hand, Mrs. Arthur Mortimer struck me as the kind of woman who just might enjoy killing anyone who she felt stood in her way, plus the fact that she certainly looked to me to be strong enough to move the body. There was something about her demeanor that made a person want to watch their back when she was around. Then there was the possibility that she had Andrew to help her.

Between the two of them, they would be able to move the body easily.

"There's something about Elinor Mortimer and Andrew Thorndike that just grates on me. I can't seem to figure it out. It's almost as if they are too much alike," I said half talking to myself, and half talking to Monica.

"I know what you mean. It's almost as if they are brother and sister," Monica added sort of off handily.

It hit me like a bolt of lightning. That was it. I pulled the car off on the side of the highway and stopped. Monica looked at me as if I had lost my mind.

"What are you doing?" she asked with a tone of slight hysteria in her voice.

"You're wonderful," I said excitedly.

I reached around behind her head and pulled her to me. I kissed her hard on the lips, and then smiled at her.

"What in the world are you talking about?"

"You said it, they are brother and sister. I'd put money on it."

"You really think so?" Monica asked as if she wasn't sure herself.

"That was what I couldn't put my finger on. Think about it. They have a lot of similar features, the color of their eyes, the color and texture of their hair, the shape of their faces and even the shape of their noses. The reason that they look so much alike is because they are brother and sister," I said with a tone of excitement.

"If you're right, what difference does it make?" she asked as she looked into my eyes.

I just stared at her for a minute. This woman could come up with some of the toughest questions at the most unlikely times. I had to take a minute to think about that one. I must have looked dumb founded to her as I put the car in gear and started on down the highway again.

What real difference could it make? All it meant was that the two couples knew each other. So why didn't they seem to want anyone else to know?

"Nick? Do you think it might be possible that they are related to Elizabeth Samuelson, or possibly Bartholomew Samuelson?"

"Where did that come from?" I asked.

"It was just a thought," she said with a note of apology in the tone of her voice.

"Well, you might very well be onto something," I said after giving it some thought. "I think we need to make a couple of stops in town. The first we need to stop at the newspaper office to see what they have in the archives. Secondly, we need to stop at the police station for background checks on the guests."

"And the third, we need to stop at a café. I could use a cup of strong black coffee," Monica suggested.

"Me, too. Let's make the coffee stop first," I replied knowing that I needed more time to think.

CHAPTER ELEVEN

We didn't have very much to say to each other the rest of the way into Sturgeon Bay. I guess she was just as deep in thought as I. There was no question that it had proven to be a rather interesting day to say the least. I was pretty sure that Monica didn't often go around finding dead bodies stuffed in crates in her normal line of work, especially recently dead people that she had sat next to during dinner. I was sure that she had seen mummies before, but that would be different. After all, she worked in the History Department.

As I drove through town, we both kept an eye out for the local newspaper office. Monica spotted it first and pointed it out to me. I pulled up in front of the newspaper office and parked the car.

I happened to glance down the street and see the little café where we had lunch and visited with Wilber Polk the other day. It was only about a half a block from where I parked.

I glanced over at Monica. She must have noticed the café, too, as she glanced over at me and smiled. It was as if she was reading my mind.

"Why not?" Monica asked. "The coffee was good and we did get some very interesting information from Wilber."

I opened the door and got out of the car. I walked around to the other side and opened the door for Monica. She reached out and took hold of my hand as I helped her out of the car. She didn't let go of my hand as we started down the sidewalk toward the café.

There were several tourists wandering around looking in the windows of the souvenir shops. There was a gentle breeze blowing in from the Green Bay side of the peninsula toward the Lake Michigan side. Although it was warm and the sun was shining, the breeze didn't set well with me. I could feel the moisture in the air and had a feeling that it might rain tonight.

Just as we turned to go into the café, the sun slipped back behind a cloud. I paused for a moment and looked up. A thick dark cloud had moved in front of the sun blocking off its light. It was the kind of cloud that could produce rain at any time, and lots of it. I wondered if it might be an omen of what was to come, even though I don't believe in omens.

We went inside and stopped for a second near the door to look around. Wilber sat across the room on his favorite stool. He had a big grin on his face. He had seen us come in. He got up and moved to a booth that was close to where he had been sitting. He motioned for us to join him. We looked at each other and agreed to sit with him, even though we hadn't said a word to each other.

"Howdy, folks," Wilber said as we slid into the booth across from him.

"Hi, Wilber," Monica said with a slight bit of a sexy tone in her voice.

"Hi, Wilber. How things been?"

"Pretty good. Say, Betty, how about a couple of cups of coffee for my friends," he called out to the woman behind the counter.

Wilber turned and looked at me.

"Say, you still interested in that Bar-thol-o-mew Samuelson fellow? You know, that ship's captain?" Wilber asked as if he was looking for some kind of a reaction.

I found it strange that Wilber would pronounce his first name like he did. It gave me the impression that he didn't like Captain Samuelson very much, but he would not have known him. After all, Captain Samuelson had most likely been dead for close to a hundred years, maybe more.

It suddenly dawned on me that Wilber must have found out something more about the captain, something that didn't sit well with Wilber's sense of values. I was instantly very much interested in what Wilber might have found out.

"Sure. You know something more about him?"

"I sure do."

Wilber looked up as Betty brought over two cups of coffee on a tray and a coffeepot to refill Wilber's cup. Wilber waited until his cup was full and he had a chance to add a heaping spoon of sugar to the coffee. He took his time and I was getting a little impatient for him to finally decide to tell us what he knew.

"Did you know that Captain Samuelson was originally from England?" he asked as he slowly stirred his coffee.

"No, we didn't know that," Monica answered as her level of interest took a quick jump up, as did mine.

"Yup. It seems the story is that he got run out of England 'cause he killed a man over there. It was over some woman, I think. Of course, he was a young man back then. They say he came here to keep from gettin' hung.

"After he got over here, he started working on the old sailin' ships out on the Great Lakes. After several years of sailin', he proves himself to be a right smart sailor. Suddenly, he ups and quits the ship he had been workin' on and becomes a ship's captain for another shippin' company out of Chicago, so they say. Shortly after that, he seemed to have a lot of money and built himself that house out on the point."

"You don't say," I replied.

So far, Wilber hadn't said anything that would lead me to believe that Captain Samuelson was anything less than what I thought him to be. He had been a man with a hot temper, worked hard to get to be a ship's captain, and probably had been a tough, stern leader who would not tolerate laziness.

"Yup. There was also some rumors that he did a little pirating on the side and that haulin' freight was just a cover. It's even been said that he stashed his loot up there at his home. I don't think no one ever proved anything, not that they didn't try."

It was this last bit of information that made me sit up and take notice. If what Wilber was saying was true, then there was a very good reason for someone to want Tom off that property. Just the thought of hidden treasure often made people do strange things. Greed was a very good motive for a lot of things, including murder.

I glanced over at Monica just as she looked over at me. It was clear by the look on her face that she was thinking the same thing I was. It also made me wonder just what was in all those old wooden crates in the mine. I had to wonder if the crates were full of pirated treasure.

"I say somethin' wrong?" Wilber asked as he looked from Monica to me.

"Not a thing, Wilber, not a thing," I said with a smile.

Monica looked at me over her cup as she sipped the warm liquid. It was clear to me that she wanted to talk, but not in front of Wilber.

I took a drink of my coffee as I thought. With this new bit of information, I couldn't help but think that there was a strong possibility that Andrew Thorndike and Elinor Mortimer knew about Samuelson's pirating activities. They either knew about the treasure, or had a strong suspicion that it existed somewhere in or around the lodge. If so, then they had a very strong motive for wanting Tom off the property. With Tom out of the way, they would be able to search for the loot without anyone disturbing them. My guess was that they knew about the treasure and wanted Tom out of the way while they removed it from the mine.

We already knew about Mr. Beresford's relationship to Elizabeth Samuelson, but what about the Thorndikes and the

Mortimers? I wondered if Elinor and Andrew might also be related to Elizabeth Samuelson, but from the other side of the family tree, perhaps.

"Wilber, do you know whatever happened to Captain Bartholomew Samuelson?" I asked.

"Don't know. I don't think anyone knows for sure. It seems he disappeared shortly after his wife disappeared. One story has it, and some folks agree, that he went back to England. Others say he went down with his ship durin' a storm on Lake Huron or Lake Erie. It seems no one can decide for sure. I'm not sure that anyone really knows what happened to him," Wilber explained.

"Do you know if Captain Samuelson had any family around here, other than Elizabeth?"

"I don't think so, but you might be able to find out at the courthouse."

"At the courthouse?" Monica asked with surprise.

"Sure. Back when Bartholomew and Elizabeth got married, they had to list the names of their parents on the Application for Marriage records. They'd be part of the records in the courthouse. You see, they was married right here in Sturgeon Bay."

That made it very clear what our next move should be. We needed to find out who was related to whom.

Wilber seemed very proud of himself and his knowledge of the area, as well he should. He had been a fountain of information and a very valuable resource to us.

"I think we need to pay another visit to Miss McGaughey at the courthouse," Monica said thoughtfully.

"Right."

"Millie McGaughey?" Wilber asked somewhat surprised at the mention of her name.

"I don't know her first name, but she is the older lady that works in the records section in the courthouse."

Wilber smiled.

"That's my Millie. We been seeing each other for close to fifteen years, now," he said proudly.

"She is a very nice lady," I commented.

"Will you be goin' over to the courthouse now?"

"Yes," I replied.

"Would you mind askin' her if she would join me here for lunch?"

"We wouldn't mind at all. We'd be happy to give her your message," Monica replied with a smile.

We quickly finished our coffee and said goodbye to Wilber. As we left the café, Monica took my hand and looked up at me with a smile. I knew there was something on her mind.

"What's going on in that pretty little head of yours?"

"I was just thinking how sweet Wilber can be when he puts his mind to it. Did you see the way his eyes lit up at the mention of Millie's name?" Monica asked.

"He likes her a lot, I'm sure."

We crossed the street and walked down the block to the courthouse. It didn't take us long to find Millie in the records room.

"Millie, isn't it?" Monica asked.

"Why, yes."

"Wilber asked us to give you a message. He would like you to join him for lunch at the café down the street."

Her eyes sparkled at the mention of Wilber's name, and she seemed a little embarrassed that we might know that they were sweethearts.

"Thank you," she replied shyly.

"Millie, I was wondering if you could help us find the marriage license for Elizabeth Beresford, Elizabeth Mae Beresford and Bartholomew Samuelson?"

"Oh, my. That was a long time ago. They didn't use marriage licenses here at that time, but they did have to make an Application for Marriage record. You see, when a couple wanted to get married, they would have to go to the courthouse and list their next of kin and who their parents were in a book kept here. They would get a little piece of paper showing that they had registered and then a preacher could perform the wedding. The preacher would have them sign the Certificate of Marriage after the wedding, then give it to them."

"Is it possible that book is still around?"

"Oh, yes. It would help if you know when they got married."

"I can only guess. It would have been about eighteen ninety or eighteen ninety-one, somewhere around that time."

"That shouldn't be too hard to find. There were not that many weddings in the early eighteen nineties around here," she replied as she started off down a long row of shelves filled with large heavy bound books.

We followed Millie into a large safe and past several more bookshelves that were lined with very official looking books. She went almost to the end of the row and began looking at the labels on the books. She stepped up on a stool and picked a large, rather heavy book off one of the upper shelves.

"I don't suppose that you know the date they were married or the date they registered?" she asked as she stepped down off the stool.

"No, I'm afraid not. We're not even sure of the year," Monica said apologetically.

"In that case, you will have to just look through the books until you find them listed," she said as she set a book down on a table.

"We appreciate all you have done. You have been a great help, Millie," I said.

"You're welcome," she replied with a slight smile. "This is the book covering eighteen ninety and ninety-one. If you need ninety-two, I will get it for you. You have a lot of searching to do, so I will leave you for now. Please call me if you need my help."

We thanked her again for all her help and began the task of finding the Application for Marriage. We turned page after page after page in the book, carefully scanning each page for their names. Although there had not been all that many marriages in the county in those two years, each page contained the information for just one Application for Marriage.

It was getting close to lunchtime before we finished with the Application for Marriage, for eighteen ninety. We were several pages into eighteen ninety-one when I saw the name Bartholomew Samuelson.

"Here it is."

Monica moved up beside me and looked over my shoulder as I carefully scanned the page. There was a list of all the names of the next of kin on both sides of each of their families. Suddenly, I spotted a familiar name under Bartholomew's parents. The father of Bartholomew was shown as Duncan Bartholomew Samuelson of London England, and his mother's maiden name was listed as Rebecca Ellen Thorndike of Whinshire, England.

"Rebecca Ellen Thorndike. I guess that shows us why the Thorndikes are here. This gives us a little more to go on," I said.

"It may give us more to go on, but what does it prove?"

Monica had a very good point. We now knew that Andrew Thorndike was very likely a relative of Bartholomew Samuelson. Since we were already convinced that Elinor Mortimer was Andrew's sister, it became clear that she was a relative as well. The question was what did it prove? As far as I could tell, it proved nothing.

There was a big difference between what we knew or thought we knew, and what we could prove. At this point, all we had was a connection to the family by a name. It was possible that it was a different family all together, but I didn't believe that for one minute.

Why were they here? What were they here for? Did they know that Bartholomew Samuelson had been a pirate? Were they here in an attempt to find his treasure or had they already found it? Were they trying to get the treasure out of the house without anyone catching them removing it?

What they were after was all speculation on our part. We had no real knowledge of their reasons for being at the lodge. We certainly didn't have any proof.

Monica suddenly interrupted my thoughts as she tapped me on the shoulder. I turned my head to look at her.

"I think we should go to the police with what we know," Monica suggested.

"And just what is it that we know?"

"We know that Priscilla Thorndike is dead."

"Yes, we do know that," I had to agree. "If we go tell the police that Elizabeth Samuelson was murdered and that Priscilla Thorndike, or whatever her actual name was, was murdered, and that the murders are connected, they're going to lock us up as a couple of full blown nuts.

"I doubt very much that we can get a judge to issue a search warrant for the mine and the lodge based on that kind of a story. He is going to want some kind of proof."

"I see your point," Monica replied disappointedly.

"There's another problem I just thought of," I said as I thought about going to the police.

"What's that?"

"What if someone has moved the body by now? We drag the police out there, and there's no body, what then?"

"I suppose they would think we are crazy."

"I suppose you're right, but we are not crazy. But aside from that, our creditability would go down the drain.

"I see your point," Monica agreed.

"What we have to do is get enough proof that the police will believe us and be able to get a warrant and search the property."

"How do we do that?" she asked.

"A very good question, but I don't have a very good answer, yet."

Monica smiled as she reached out and took hold of my hand.

"You are crazy, but I like you."

"I like you, too," I said as I leaned over and kissed her lightly on the cheek.

"Well, what do we do now?" she said with a deep sigh.

I thought for a second before replying. "I think that we should go back to the lodge. I would like to find a way into the icehouse and hopefully from the icehouse to the mine. I've got a feeling that the mine is connected to the icehouse. We might be able to figure out who knows about it, or maybe even find a clue that would lead us to who killed Mrs. Thorndike. We also might be able to find out who is trying to get Tom off the property."

Monica looked at me with those beautiful cobalt blue eyes. I was sure that she still wanted to go to the police, but she could see the results of such a move without any proof to back up our story. She simply closed the book and took my hand as we turned and left the courthouse.

CHAPTER TWELVE

We walked out of the courthouse and down the street to where we had left Monica's car. I held the door for her as she got in. Once I was in the car, I started it and pulled out onto the highway. We left Sturgeon Bay and hurried back to the lodge.

Neither of us seemed to have very much to say. I knew Monica was disappointed that we had not gone to the police, but I also knew that she understood why we didn't.

We arrived back at the lodge just a few minutes after twelve o'clock. We went directly into the dining room where we found the guests already seated. Mr. and Mrs. Arthur Mortimer, the newlyweds, Andrew Thorndike and Tom were all looking at us when we came into the dining room. Mr. Beresford was not there and I had to wonder why.

"Please excuse us for being late," I said but decided not to offer an explanation.

I pulled a chair out and held it for Monica. After she was seated, I sat down beside her and scooted up to the table. I noticed that Arthur Mortimer was sitting across the table from me. He sat with his hands folded in front of him and his head tipped down as if he was examining the empty plate in front of him. I can't remember ever seeing a man who appeared to be so beaten down, so completely whipped. He looked discouraged and afraid.

Elinor Mortimer was sitting across from Monica. She was looking across the table at me with those hard cold eyes of hers. It was almost as if she was daring me to talk to Arthur. I also got the impression that she was trying to look into my head in the hope of finding out what I was thinking, or possibly to find out just how much I knew about her and

Andrew. Her jaw drew tight and the skin around her neck and temples took on a reddish tinge when I looked her right in eyes and grinned at her. She quickly looked away.

"You almost missed lunch," Tom said as he passed a platter full of chicken to Arthur Mortimer.

"We're sorry about that, but we were in town on a couple of errands," Monica replied as she passed me the plate with the ears of corn neatly stacked on it.

I took an ear of corn, set it on my plate and passed the serving dish on to Andrew Thorndike. I couldn't help but wonder what he was thinking at this moment. He looked as if he didn't have a care in the world, as if nothing was wrong.

"Andrew, it is Andrew isn't it?"

"Yes, it is," he replied rather begrudgingly.

It was clear that he didn't want to talk to me, or anyone else for that matter. By the same token, I was not going to let him get away without explaining to everyone seated at the table why his wife was not sitting here with the rest of us.

"Well, Andrew, I see your wife is not with us. I hope she isn't feeling poorly," I said as I passed him the chicken.

He looked at me with a slight glare in his eyes and then said, "She is simply resting."

His reply was said flatly, making it clear by the tone of his voice and the look in his eyes that it was none of my business where his wife was. This guy was good. His response was smooth and restrained, showing not the slightest hint of a lie. Except for his cold, dark, penetrating eyes, there was no sign of any kind of emotion from him at all.

All I could think was that sitting next to me was a man who could kill and not think twice about it. I wondered if his sister on the other side of the table was equally as cold blooded and callous. From what little I had heard through the walls of my room, there was no doubt in my mind that she could kill just as easily.

I looked back toward Tom and noticed that he seemed to look as if he might have gotten some rest lately. There was better color in his face and he seemed more alive. I hoped to get a chance to talk to him after lunch.

"Mr. Mortimer - -, Arthur," I said.

Arthur's head snapped up as if it were on a very tight spring, and by saying his name I had released the catch. Speaking his name had startled him so much that he dropped his fork. It bounced off the plate and fell to the floor.

"I'm sorry, sir. I didn't mean to startle you."

He quickly looked toward his wife, then at me. His eyes were like that of a basset hound, sad and lonely. The look on his face gave me the impression that he was pleading with me not to draw him into any kind of a conversation. It was clear to me that the last thing he wanted was to have me bring any attention to him.

"It's all right, Mr. McCord. Arthur has not been himself lately," Mrs. Mortimer quickly inserted before he had a chance to speak. "We came up here so that he could rest, and to give him the opportunity to recover. Please excuse us."

I watched as she stood up, took him by the arm and led him out of the room. He glanced back at me. The look on his face reminded me of a little boy who was being taken away from the table because he had been a bad boy and knew he was going to be punished.

As I watched him disappear into the other room, I had to wonder just what it was he was supposed to be recovering from. He appeared to be so frail and weak that I couldn't help but feel sorry for him. I even wished that I had not said anything to him.

Shortly after the Mortimers left, Thorndike got up and left the room. I would have liked to know where he went, but I needed to stay and talk with Tom. Within a few minutes, the newlyweds left, leaving Tom, Monica and myself sitting at the table.

"Tom, you look like you've been sleeping better."

"I have, except for last night."

"What happened last night?" I asked.

"Last night I heard that strange sound again. It's the first time since you got here that I've heard it. Otherwise, I've been able to sleep all night."

"That's great," Monica added.

"What was the sound you heard?" I asked.

"I really don't know how to describe it. It was sort of like a scraping noise, - - kind of like, - ah - - something being dragged across a - a cement floor, or something," he tried to explain.

I thought about what he had said. I didn't remember hearing anything unusual last night, but then I'm a very sound sleeper once I get to sleep. I would have to think about that later, right now I had other things on my mind.

"Tom, are you aware that there's an icehouse attached to this house?"

"Sure. We use it to store meats and other things that we want to keep frozen. It's fantastic. You know that it will keep meats frozen almost as well as an electric freezer?"

"Who else knows about the icehouse, besides you?"

"I don't know," he said as he thought for a second. "My cook and his helper, I guess."

"Anyone else?"

"Not that I know of, but then anyone could figure it out. Why?"

"We think we know who is trying to get you out of here and why. The only thing is, we can't prove it," I explained.

"Who is it?" he asked as he leaned forward.

"I'd rather not say, just yet. I need to have some proof before I say anything more."

I preferred not to say too much to Tom for two reasons. First of all, if he was a part of it, I didn't want him to know everything Monica and I knew. Secondly, if he was not a part of it, we didn't want him letting the cat out of the bag before I decided how we would catch the cat once it was out in the open.

"How do you get to the icehouse?" I asked.

"Through the basement, of course."

"Is there more than one way in or out of the icehouse?"

Monica glanced over at me as she waited to hear Tom's answer. I could see that Tom was thinking about it.

"I only know of one way in or out of the icehouse and that's through the basement. However, there are two ways into the basement. One through the kitchen, and one through a door under the stairs in the main room," he said without hesitation.

I looked at Monica. This little bit of information came as a big surprise. I knew the cook had a room off the kitchen where he lived, and that room was right next to the basement stairs. Having another way into the basement would make it easier for someone to slip into the basement without having to worry about waking the cook.

"I don't remember seeing any door under the stairs," I remarked.

"There isn't really a door as such. It's one of the panels on the wall that opens to a stairway to the basement. I found it by accident one day while I was remodeling. I don't use it, but I couldn't see any reason to block it off, either. I don't think anyone else even knows it's there. You want to go down in the basement?" he asked.

"No, not right now. Maybe some other time."

"Nick, have you figured out where the strange sounds are coming from?"

His question was a simple one, but the expression on his face told me that he was really concerned about it. His eyes pleaded for an answer.

"Not yet, but I'll figure it out," I assured him.

"I hope I have been some help."

"You have, Tom," Monica said with a pleasant smile.

"I do have some work to do, so unless I can help you some more, I'd better get to work. We can talk again later if you wish."

"Sure, Tom," I replied only half listening to him.

My mind was racing as I thought about the sounds Tom had been hearing. Why would they have all of a sudden started up again, unless whoever was making the noises was sure that only Tom would hear them? There was also the possibility that whoever was making the noises did not know that Tom could hear them.

As Tom stood up and left the dining room, I looked over at Monica. She was sitting there patiently waiting for me to say something, or to make the next move.

"What now?" she asked.

I didn't have the slightest idea. We had been able to come up with a few more pieces to the puzzle, but not enough to know what the whole picture should look like.

"I don't know. It just isn't making any sense," I said as I stared across the room at the wall.

"I have an idea."

"What's your idea? I'm pretty much open to anything right now."

"Let's go get our swimsuits on and find a nice place where we can relax and then we can talk about it," she suggested.

"That's a good idea," I replied as I stood up and held her chair.

I took her by the hand as we left the dining room. On our way upstairs, I took a quick glance around the main room. The room was empty. When we got to my room, I unlocked the door and opened it for her. We went inside and shut the door.

"I'd like to check out your room before you go in. Do you mind?" I asked.

"Not at all. After what happened last night, I'm more than happy to let you make sure that no one is in my room."

She stood back as I opened the door between our rooms. I went inside and looked around. There was no one in the room, and the room seemed to be in good order.

"It looks clear," I said as I looked around her room.

"Thank you. Would you mind if I leave the door open? I'm a little afraid to be left alone."

"Not at all."

I left her in her room while I returned to my room. I stripped out of my clothes, found my swim trunks and put them on. I was slipping into a pair of tennis shoes just as she stepped into the doorway between our rooms. She was holding a beach robe in her out stretched hand. She struck a very sexy pose while leaning against the door jam.

"Well?" she asked with a soft smile.

She was a dream to look at. She was standing in the doorway wearing a black string bikini. It did nothing to hide the smooth flowing lines of her well-proportioned body. In fact, it did nothing to hide anything. It took me a minute to get my eyes back in my head and to say something.

"I prefer just a towel, although for the life of me, I can't think of why right now," I said.

"You're sweet, but I don't think we would make it past the front door if I had nothing on but a skimpy towel," she replied with a grin.

"You wouldn't make it past my door."

"Mmmmm, that sounds exciting," she said as she stepped up in front of me and handed me her beach robe.

I took hold of the robe and held it out in front of me. She turned around and slipped into it. I grabbed a beach towel from the dresser as I followed her to the door.

After securing the door to my room, we went downstairs. Again, I glanced around the main room, but saw no one. We left the lodge and walked out toward the beach. As soon as we were walking in the sand, we turned and started down the beach away from the lodge.

We hadn't gone very far when we came upon a small cove. The water was a deep blue and clear. The bright sun reflected off the gentle ripples on the water.

"How's this?" Monica asked.

"Nice, very nice," I replied as I looked at her.

"Not me, the cove," she said with a grin.

"Oh, that's nice, too."

I picked out a spot and laid out the beach towel on the warm sand, Monica removed her beach robe and dropped it on the sand next to the towel. She knelt down on the towel, reached behind her back and untied the top of her bikini. After untying it from behind her neck, she dropped it on top of her robe and then laid down on her stomach on the towel. She crossed her arms and laid her head on her arms, then watched me.

I let my eyes wonder over her body for a moment before I laid down on my side next her and looked at her beautiful face. Her light complexion, blue eyes and blond hair made her look like no other woman I had ever known. I reached over and touched the smooth skin of her back, slowly letting my fingers gently glide along her spine.

"Nick, what are you thinking about?"

"You, what else?" I replied.

"I thought we came out here to relax and discuss what was going on at the lodge?"

"That's right, but it was your suggestion that we wear swimsuits. I expected you to do just that, wear it."

"Would you prefer that I put my top back on?"

"No. I prefer you just as you are."

She smiled at me as I rolled over on my back and looked up at the blue sky. I turned my thoughts to the lodge and the people who were staying there. I didn't say anything for several minutes.

"I saw the way you looked at me when Tom mentioned that there are two ways into the basement," she said.

"Yeah, I didn't know there were two ways to the basement. But I guess it doesn't really matter."

"Oh. You look confused." Monica said.

"I'm confused," I replied thoughtfully.

"About what?"

"It seems that we are getting almost too much information in one instance and not enough in another. It's almost as if someone is going out of their way to muddy the water, to confuse the issues," I said thoughtfully.

"I don't understand what you're talking about."

I rolled over on my side and reached out to her. I gently ran my finger over the skin on her shoulder blade as I decided just what to say and how to say it. Her skin was soft and warm from the sun.

"Well, to start with, take the police reports. Where are the test results on the body to confirm how long it had been frozen? I'm sure that they could have come up with a closer time frame than what they came up with? Yet, we have test after test after test done by the police trying to determine the cause of death, and they found nothing.

"Why wasn't a better investigation of the body done by the police to determine who she was? Yet, we have a dozen pictures of Elizabeth Samuelson right here in the lodge that were taken within the last couple of years before her death. Pictures that could easily help identify her.

"Why weren't people that are related to Elizabeth interviewed by the police? Hell, if we found out who they are, why couldn't the police?"

"I see what you mean. Do you think the police are involved in a cover-up?" she asked.

"No, not really. There may have been one or two individuals in the police department that might have been sloppy in their work or failed to get the kind of expertise that they should have, but I doubt there was any kind of a cover-up," I said as I thought about it.

"If someone in the crime lab didn't want her identified, that person or persons could just not request the experts that were needed or just not make an effort to identify the body. Is that right?"

"Yeah, pretty much," I replied as I wondered what she was getting at.

"So if there was a cover up, wouldn't there have to be someone working in the crime lab to pull it off?" Monica asked.

"Yes. It would take someone in the crime lab to pull it off. And if that were the case, that would help explain why there were no lab reports that would show whose body it was, or how long it had been in the ice. But on the other hand, and the more likely reasons might be that someone was just plain careless, or there was a lack of interest in finding out who the hundred year old corpse was on the part of the police.

"After a hundred years or more, whoever murdered Elizabeth was dead, too. So what difference could it make now? That could explain the lack of interest on the part of the police. That and the fact this little police department doesn't have the resources or money needed to solve a case that old, especially one that there would be no one to prosecute."

"I see your point. What about Mrs. Thorndike?" Monica asked.

"What about her?"

"Why do you think she was murdered?"

"My guess would be that she got scared when I showed up. I think whoever killed her was afraid that she would spill the beans. If she even hinted to the wrong person that there was something of a suspicious nature going on at the lodge, a new investigation might be started. That would have the place crawling with police again, and I don't think our killer or killers would want that," I explained.

Monica thought for a minute before commenting.

"That makes sense. You know, I have been thinking. All the guests here at the lodge have something to do with Elizabeth Samuelson, except for possibly the newlyweds. We don't know anything about them, but everyone else at the lodge is related to Elizabeth or Captain Samuelson, or they are here because of one of them."

It was strange that she should have said that at that very moment. I was beginning to think the same thing. The only difference was I was beginning to wonder why a young newly married couple would have come to this lodge at all. I had seen the advertising for the lodge and knew that Tom had been catering to older wealthy couples. He had been advertising the lodge as a place to come and relax in the old world charm of an over hundred year old house in a secluded wooded area on Lake Michigan.

"Do you know the names of the newlyweds?" I asked.

"No. I don't think I have ever heard their names mentioned."

"I think we should find out who they are, don't you?"

"Do you think they might be involved, too?" Monica asked.

"No. I don't think so. I think they came up here because this is a very secluded place where they could do just what they have been doing, swim and play on the beach in the nude," I answered as I thought about the other day when we saw them on the beach.

"You really think so?" she asked.

"Yes, but I think we should still look into it, don't you?"

"I guess so," she said as she relaxed and closed her eyes.

I gently rubbed her back as my mind wandered off to the things that had happened since I arrived at Gill's Point Lodge. Everything that had happened since I arrived seemed to point back to something that happened over a hundred years ago. It seemed that the death of Elizabeth was connected to everything else.

Question after question kept coming to mind, but the one question that still haunted me was the one I had come here to answer. Who was trying to drive Tom crazy, or at least drive him away from the lodge? It was the only question that I couldn't come up with at least one possible answer. All the other questions I could come up with had at least one plausible answer, even if I couldn't prove my answer to be correct. In some cases, I could come up with more than one possible answer.

I rolled over onto my back, closed my eyes and let my thoughts tramp around in the back of my mind for a little while. I began to search the deep recesses of my mind for anything that might lead me to an answer, but I always seemed to come up empty.

I suddenly felt a warm hand lightly brush across my chest and come to rest on my shoulder. I opened my eyes to see Monica propped up on her elbows looking down at me with those beautiful blue eyes. I could feel the warmth of her breasts brush lightly against my skin as she moved closer to me.

With her lips only inches from mine, she whispered, "If you don't kiss me, I'll - - -."

She didn't get a chance to finish her sentence. I was not about to let a chance like this slip by without some kind of a positive response. I wrapped my arms around her and pulled her over me.

Our lips met in a long, deep passionate kiss. Her firm bare breasts pressing against my chest and her warm soft lips pressing against mine made me forget all the questions that had been filling my mind just moments ago.

As my hand slid lightly over the smooth skin of her back, I lost all consciousness of my surroundings. For us, we were alone and we were the only people in the world. For us, there was no world except for this tiny world that we had created right here on a beach towel spread out on this little piece of sandy beach.

As we kissed passionately, we rolled over on our sides. I let my hand slid up between us and onto one of her firm breasts. She moaned softly as I gently slid the palm of my hand across her nipple. I then slid my hand off her breast and down her side to her hip. Holding her tightly against me in a passionate kiss, my fingers carefully untied the side of her bikini and let it fall away from her hip.

She let out a soft sigh as I gently moved my hand over her hip. She curled her leg over mine as I let my hand slide down over her firm behind and down onto the back of her leg. The texture of her skin and smoothness of the flowing lines of her body consumed me. I rose up and looked into her eyes. Her passion was clearly visible in those beautiful cobalt blue eyes. I leaned down to kiss her again and we were lost in our deep passionate love for each other.

CHAPTER THIRTEEN

I laid quietly on my back looking up at the clear blue sky. Monica was lying at my side with the warmth of her firm breasts pressing against me, and her arm lying across my chest. Her soft blond hair cascaded over my shoulder where she laid her head. The smoothness of her leg against mine helped to complete the feeling of contentment that had filled me. Her nude body was so close to me that it did little to bring me back to reality.

As I lay there, I watched several small birds fly overhead. I could hear the sound of a gentle breeze rustling the leaves of the nearby trees. There were also the sounds of birds singing in the woods. All in all, it was a perfect day that I was not likely to forget, ever.

Suddenly, I felt her stir ever so slightly and wondered if she was ready to get up or if she would prefer to lie in the sun for a little while longer. The sun was growing warm on my skin and I knew it would not take long before we could get a little sunburned.

"Would you like to go for a swim?" she asked softly without lifting her head from my shoulder.

"If you'd like," I replied and kissed her lightly on the top of her head.

She raised her head up, looked down at me and smiled.

"I hate to be a party pooper, but I don't think I should spend too much more time out in the sun. I burn rather easily."

It was easy to see that with her fair complexion, she would not be able to stay out in the sun very long, but that was okay with me. I was never one for spending a lot of time lying around in the sun anyway. I was ready for a brief swim and then move the blanket up onto the grass in the shade of a large oak tree. With the sun so bright and no clouds to cool its rays, it was getting very hot as it often does in the mid-afternoon this time of year.

"I'm ready for a swim. All I need to know is if that is with or without swimsuits?" I asked playfully.

"Without, of course," she answered with a smile. "It was you who suggested that we spend an afternoon on the beach like the newlyweds," she reminded me.

"Not a bad suggestion, was it?"

"No, not bad at all," she replied as she leaned over me and kissed me lightly on the lips.

After a warm and tender kiss, Monica rolled onto her back as I slipped my arm out from behind her. I sat up and looked over my shoulder at her. I wasn't sure if the glow of her body was due to the hot afternoon sun, or from the passion for each other that we had shared only moments ago.

"You are beautiful," I said in a hushed whisper.

"So are you," she said as she sat up beside me.

She leaned over against me and kissed me lightly. There was no doubt in my mind that this woman was special, very special. Being totally nude with her felt as natural as watching the sun rise in the morning or set in the evening.

I stood up and reached down to her. She took hold of my hands and I pulled her up on her feet. As she stepped up in front of me, she let go of my hands, reached up and put her hands on my shoulders. She smiled up at me as she pressed her body against me and tipped her head back. Wrapping my arms around her, I leaned down to kiss her. I pulled her tightly against me as we kissed. It was a long passionate kiss that caused us to breathe hard, and to revel in each other's warmth.

Taking a break in order for us to catch our breath, she leaned back a little and looked up at me. The soft smile on her face and the sparkle in her eyes made it easy for me to see that she liked being held close. There was no doubt in my mind that I liked holding her close to me.

"I think a little swim might be a good idea," she whispered softly.

"I could use a little cooling off, too," I said as I smiled down at her.

Her soft smile quickly turned to a broad grin. She under-stood clearly the meaning of my comment and gave me a quick kiss. Taking her arms from around my neck, she grabbed my hand and began leading me toward the water. As we approached the lake, we sort of ran the last few feet of the beach and out into the waters of Lake Michigan.

As soon as we were out where it was deep enough to swim, I let go of her hand and dove into the water. She must have followed my lead as she came up right beside me. Neither of us stayed under water very long. In fact, we came up rather quickly as the cold water washed over our warm naked bodies.

"Damn, this is cold," I said as I stood up and pushed my hair back away from my eyes.

It had been a long time since I had been swimming in Lake Michigan. I had forgotten how cold the water could be this time of year.

"Feels good once you get acclimated to it," she said with a smile.

"Well, I'm not too sure I want to get 'acclimated' to it," I replied as I moved closer to her.

We enjoyed our time together just splashing around and holding onto each other in the water. However, it didn't take very long before we had enough of the cold water and began to shiver. We had long since rinsed off the sweat and we were ready to get out. Hand in hand we walked out of the lake and up onto the beach.

When we got back to our beach towel, I simply stood in the sun and let the sun warm me a little before I reached down and picked up my swimsuit. As I stepped into my swimsuit, I watched Monica put her string bikini on. Somehow, she looked as sexy with it on as she had without it, but that may have been due to the fact that it covered so little of her.

As soon as we were dressed, I gathered up the beach towel. We walked back off the beach to a shady spot on the thick grass under a large oak tree. I laid out the beach towel next to an old dead tree that had fallen many years ago. All its bark had dried and fallen off. I sat down on the towel and leaned back against the smooth weather beaten log.

Monica laid down on her back and rested her head in my lap. I ran my hand through her hair as I looked her over.

She smiled up at me and whispered, "What are you thinking?"

"I was thinking about how sexy and beautiful you are."

"Thank you," she replied as she took hold of my hand and laid it on her stomach.

She closed her eyes and seemed to relax. I took my clue from her and tipped my head back against the log, then closed my eyes. It felt good to just be in the cool of the shade with her. At that moment, I could not think of one single place that I would rather be.

The quietness of the moment was disturbed when Monica said, "I was thinking about the newlyweds again. If the newlyweds are related to Elizabeth, how do they fit into the picture?"

I opened my eyes and looked down at her. She was looking up at me and waiting for an answer.

"I'm not convinced that they are a part of any of this, or that they are related to anyone here. They seem to be gone most of the time. The few times that I have seen them, they have been falling all over each other."

"True, but have you noticed that they are the only ones that we rarely see?"

"But we did see them on the beach in their nothings. I doubt if they planned on being seen," I replied, wondering what she was getting at.

"That's true, but we had already left the house. If they thought we were going into town, why stay around and watch for us? I'm sure that they were convinced that we would be gone for several hours at least."

"What are you getting at?" I asked.

"Well, we never saw them just before we saw someone in the tower. You thought you saw a man, I thought I saw a women on one occasion. You think it's possible that they are the ones we have been seeing in the tower?"

I thought for a moment before I replied.

"I suppose it's possible, but why?"

"Let's assume that they are related to the others for a minute. That means that we're the only ones, other than Tom, who are not related to either Elizabeth or Captain Samuelson in some way. If they are related to the others, maybe their part in this is to keep an eye on us whenever we're around the lodge."

I had to think about what she was saying. It was possible that they were keeping an eye on us, but for whom?

"That's an interesting thought, accept for the fact that no one knew I was coming here, except Tom," I replied. "However, I do agree that it would still be a good idea if we check them out tomorrow."

I tipped my head back to relax again. It was too late to go into town and check on the newlyweds now so that would have to wait for another time. The courthouse would be closed by the time we could get there. Besides I had other things to think about right now, like how was I going to get into the basement of the lodge without anyone seeing me.

The more I thought about it, the more I was convinced that the easiest and safest way into the basement was through the door in the main room. There was always the possibility that someone might be watching the secret entrance, but the kitchen entrance didn't offer a much better solution.

Getting past the cook without waking him seemed a little too risky. I didn't know the cook well enough to know what kind of sleeper he might be. If he was a light sleeper, it could prove very difficult getting by him without disturbing him. It was going to be difficult no matter which way I used to get to the basement.

I had almost forgotten that my hand was resting on Monica's stomach. I suddenly felt her warm soft hand slide over my hand. I leaned forward and looked down to find Monica looking up at me.

"You are not going into the icehouse without me," she said, as she looked me right in the eyes.

This woman was not only beautiful, but she knew what I was thinking. I really didn't mind because a good part of the time I was thinking about her.

"It could get a little tricky, even dangerous," I warned.

"I have been working with you on this from the time you arrived. If you will recall, I was even here first. I'm not going to let you continue without me," she said.

Her words had the meaning of a threat, but the tone of her voice indicated more of a plea for me not to leave her behind. Even those sparkling blue eyes of hers pleaded with me to take her along. There was no doubt in my mind that she was one determined woman.

"Tonight, WE will find our way into the basement and then on into the icehouse," I said reassuringly.

She smiled up at me as she squeezed my hand. Even though I had assured her that she would be a part of going into the basement, I was still a little concerned about involving her in the search of the basement and icehouse. As I said, it could be dangerous and there was no telling what we might find. There was always the possibility that we might encounter someone who might be a little less than friendly, someone like Elinor Mortimer.

I leaned my head back against the log again and began to mentally make plans for tonight. We spent a major part of the afternoon in the shade of the big trees just resting and being close to each other.

It had been a very relaxing and pleasant afternoon, but it had gone by rather quickly. We returned to the lodge about an hour before dinner, plenty of time to get cleaned up. After showering and dressing for dinner, we met in the main room.

Monica arrived in the main room first. I came down shortly after her. She had picked out a quiet corner where we could see everyone who came into the room or went into the dining room.

Sitting in one corner of the main room was Mr. Beresford. He seemed to be very engrossed in what appeared to be a very old book, or possibly an old journal. He seemed to be studying it very intently. He glanced up, over the top of the book and saw me. Although our eyes met, he didn't acknowledge my presence. He quickly looked away and returned to his reading as if he were afraid someone might catch him looking my way.

"Look," Monica whispered as she looked toward the staircase.

I looked up and saw Elinor Mortimer coming down the stairs. I quickly picked up on what Monica had noticed. Elinor Mortimer was alone. Her husband was not with her. The first thought that passed through my mind was to wonder if Mr. Mortimer had met the same fate as Mrs. Thorndike.

"I wonder where Mr. Mortimer is?" Monica asked in a whisper almost as if she had been reading my mind.

"I don't know. I hope he's not with Mrs. Thorndike."

I heard a faint sigh of relief from Monica when Mr. Mortimer suddenly appeared at the top of the stairs. It was clear that Monica had been worried about Mr. Mortimer. I must admit that I was a little relieved to see him, too.

"I guess that answers that question," I said softly.

The next ones down the stairs were the newlyweds. They were arm in arm, and the woman was leaning against the man as if she could not get close enough to him. The more I observed them, the more I wondered about them. Their open affection for each other seemed almost as if it was a game, an act played out for the benefit of the rest of us.

As they walked by, the woman looked over at me, smiled and winked. It was sort of a sexy smile, as if she was trying to get me to react to her flirting with me. I had to admit that she was a sexy young woman to look at, but definitely not my type. Certainly not nearly as sexy or as beautiful as Monica.

"She is flirting with you," Monica said with a tone of astonishment. "I thought she was so wrapped up in her new husband that she couldn't even see another man."

I seemed to hear a slight note of jealousy in Monica's voice, but what really struck me as strange was the fact that this woman would flirt with anyone. Then it came to me. I had to ask myself if she was flirting with me or if she was letting me know that she knew we had been watching them?

"I don't think she was flirting with me," I said as I looked at Monica.

"What? You don't call that flirting?"

I could see a little fire in Monica's eyes. It felt kind of good to know that there was someone who cared enough about me to be jealous.

"I think it was just her way of telling us that she knew that we have been watching them, and that we were watching them just a little too intently to suit her," I said with a grin.

"You mean it was her way of saying, "take a picture it'll last longer"?" Monica asked, looking at me as she wondered if I was kidding her or not.

"Something like that, but probably more like, 'mind our own damn business'. I don't think she likes us watching them so closely."

"Do you think they are involved?"

"Involved? Only in each other," I replied with a grin. "I don't think they have anything to do with anything, except themselves."

Just then Tom came out of the dining room and invited everyone to come in and sit down for dinner. We followed the rest of the guests into the dining room and sat down. Mr. and Mrs. Mortimer sat across the table from us and Mr. Beresford sat down near the end of the table. Tom sat at the head of the table and the newlyweds sat to my left. The only one that was not at the table was Andrew Thorndike.

Once we were all seated, Tom started passing the food around the table. Mr. Thorndike arrived late and sat down near the end of the table.

"I'm sorry to be late, but Mrs. Thorndike is still feeling poorly. I sat with her for a few minutes before coming down to make sure she was as comfortable as possible."

This guy was smooth, I thought. He sat there and lied through his teeth without so much as a flinch of an eyelash. I wondered how long he would be able to keep up this masquerade, although I was sure that he felt that no one would ever find Mrs. Thorndike.

"I'm sorry to hear that she is still feeling poorly. Is there anything we can do?" Monica asked.

"Yes, what can we do to make her more comfortable?" Tom added.

"She is quite comfortable, right now. I think the best thing we can do for her is to let her rest and remain undisturbed," he replied politely.

I'll bet she's comfortable, and I sure as hell bet that you don't want her disturbed, I thought. She's dead, and how much more comfortable can you get than dead. And if she was disturbed, it could mean a lot of trouble for Andrew.

Then it hit me. It would be almost impossible to keep up the pretext for very long without causing a great deal of suspicion, especially since we all eat together. This man was not stupid. He was going to have to make some kind of a move, and make it soon. I got the feeling that whatever his reason for being here, he would try to finish up and get out of here before his wife was discovered.

As I ate, I continued to observe the rest of the guests as casually as possible. We finished dinner in relative quiet, no one speaking to anyone else after our little exchange about his wife. When dinner was over, everyone left the dining room without so much as a single word.

Monica and I went out to the main room and sat down at the small table next to the stairs. We played a little rummy, but I found it hard to concentrate on the game. I tried to examine the panels along the wall as discreetly as possible in an effort to figure out which one would open up to the basement.

Looking down at the carpet at the base of one of the panels, I noticed that the carpet had been brushed in sort of quarter circle. It started up against the wall and fanned out into the room. It was apparent that the panel that opened to the basement swung out into the room.

"It's getting late and I'm tired. I think I will go to bed," I said to Monica.

At first, she looked at me with a look of wonder in her eyes. It was still early and everyone, except the newlyweds, were sitting around trying to look unconcerned about what the others were doing. It took her just a couple of seconds to pick up on what was going on in my head.

"Me, too," she replied.

I stacked the cards neatly on the table and then stood up. I reached out a hand to Monica. She took my hand, stood up and then walked with me to the stairs.

As we climbed the stairs, I made sure that I stepped on the third step from the top. I wanted to be sure that the others in the main room were aware that the third step creaked when stepped on. That way, whoever it was who was trying to keep track of us would listen for it. If they didn't hear it creak, they might think that we were still in our rooms.

We went directly to my room. As we entered the room, I glanced down the hall to see if anyone else had followed us up the stairs. The hall was clear; there was no one behind us. I shut the door and locked it.

CHAPTER FOURTEEN

Once we were in my room and had the door closed, Monica and I immediately changed into dark clothes and soft-soled shoes before we settling down on the bed to rest and wait. I had gathered the flashlights and made sure that everything was in order in preparations for our search of the basement. There was nothing left to do but to relax and wait until the time was right.

Time seemed to pass at a snail's pace as we waited for everyone to go to their rooms for the night, and for the house to get quiet. We also had to give everyone an opportunity to get to sleep before we started our search.

I sat in the dark leaning back against the headboard with Monica curled up along side me. She rested her head in my lap as she caught a few winks.

During the hours of waiting, my mind began to wander through all the information that we had discovered about this place and the people who had lived here. Although we had been told that the lodge had been built as the summer home for the very beautiful Elizabeth Samuelson, and that it was one of the most beautiful houses out on the point; it had a rather dark and mysterious history. The question that continued to haunt me was, had it really been built for the lovely Elizabeth, or had it been built as a place to hide the bounty that Captain Samuelson stole from other ships on the lakes? From what I had seen so far, I was convinced that it had been built as a place to hide the captain's bounty.

I glanced over at the clock on the dresser and saw that it was about half past one in the morning. It had been well over two hours since I had heard any doors open or close, or heard any water running, or any other sounds that could be caused by people moving about the lodge. I felt that it was a good time for us to get up and start our search. We had to be done with our search of the basement well before the cook got up to start preparing for breakfast.

"Monica, - - - honey," I said softly in an effort to wake her, but not startle her.

"Hmmm?" she replied.

"It's time," I whispered.

"Oh."

Reluctantly, she raised her head off my lap and rolled over on her back. Wiping the sleep from her eyes, she stretched her muscles to get them to wake up. She turned away from me and swung her legs off the side of the bed as she sat up. I reached over and gently kneaded her shoulders to help take a little of the stiffness out of them.

"That feels good," she whispered.

"You ready?" I asked.

She nodded in reply. I got off the bed and walked around to the other side. Picking up our jackets from the chair, I handed her a jacket and slipped into my own. As she stood up, I gave her one of the flashlights.

"We have to be very quiet," I whispered as we moved toward the door. "Remember, the third step from the top of the stairs creaks when you step on it. Be sure not to step on it."

"Which way are we going to use to get into the basement?"

"I thought about using the one off the kitchen, but I don't want anyone knowing that we are down there. I don't know the cook well enough to know what kind of a sleeper he is. We could wake the cook if we go through the kitchen. I think it will be better if we use the entrance to the basement off the main room."

"Do you think it might be watched?"

"It's possible, but at this hour, probably not," I replied. "All we have to do is figure out how to get the panel to open."

The concerned look on Monica's face indicated that she had not considered the possibility that the panel would not simply open when we pushed on it. I smiled at her in an effort to reassure her that we could open it, although I wasn't all that sure myself.

I turned around and walked to the door of my room. Monica stood behind me as I carefully unlocked the door and slowly turned the knob. I had checked it out earlier. The door worked smoothly, and I was able to open it without a sound. Once we were out in the hall, I closed the door carefully, but decided not to take the chance of making any noise by locking it.

Slowly and quietly, we worked our way down the hall to the stairs. As I started down the stairs, I silently reminded Monica of the noisy step by pointing at it and stepping over it. She followed my lead by stepping over the noisy step.

We kept our flashlights in our jacket pockets. The dim glow of the night-lights provided enough light for us to see our way down the stairs and around the main room. After making sure that there was no one else in the main room, we went to the panel below the stairs.

I had no idea how to get the panel to open, but I was reasonably sure that there was some kind of latch or hook hidden in the fancy molding. I moved the chair from in front of the wall panel and began checking along the molding for some kind of catch or fastener. I soon discovered a small latch hidden behind a curve in the delicate molding. As I released the latch, the door opened very slightly, only a few inches. Not enough to slip by. I carefully pulled the door open, just far enough to allow us to squeeze through.

Monica stood at my elbow while I took a minute to check it out. I turned toward her, backed away from the door and nudged her gently toward it. She glanced at me and then stepped up to the door.

"Use your flashlight, but keep it pointed down toward the basement," I whispered softly.

She took her flashlight from her pocket, pointed it through the door toward the basement and turned it on. There was a small landing just inside the entrance. She stepped inside onto the landing and waited for me to join her.

I took a quick look around the main room to make sure that we had not been seen before stepping onto the landing. I then slowly pulled the door closed behind me, being careful not to make any noise. I turned on my flashlight and shined it around before venturing any further. I wanted to be sure that the steps were safe before we started down them.

Taking hold of the railing, I started down the stairs. I moved slowly, being careful to make as little noise as possible. Monica had her hand on my shoulder and followed close behind. We were able to reach the bottom of the stairs with only the slight creaking of two or three of the steps. When we got to the bottom, I stopped and took a look around shining my flashlight slowly around the basement.

The large old beams that supported the old house were full of cobwebs and dust. The wooden steps that led to the basement were covered with years of dust and dirt. However, when I examined them more closely with the help of my flashlight, I could see that the dust had been disturbed on every step. It was clear that someone, other than us, had been using these stairs and not very long ago. In fact, the stairway had obviously been used several times recently. All that did was confirm what I already suspected. Someone was using this way to get to the basement, then on to the icehouse.

I continued to inspect the rest of the basement. The basement appeared to be very typical of the basements of most of these old homes. The floor was made of flat smooth stones laid very carefully to make the floor as smooth and as even as possible. The walls of the basement were made of granite stones neatly cut, shaped and stacked with thick layers of mortar between them.

The ceiling was low, barely more then six foot high, with large heavy beams supporting the thick wooden floor above. Heavy vertical rough cut posts supported the beams at regular intervals. The air had the faint smell of mildew and was stale. There was very little air circulation.

"Nick, look over here," Monica whispered as she touched my arm.

I turned around and looked in the direction that the beam of her flashlight was pointing. There in the corner, half hidden by the stairs and a large brown tarp were two fair sized wooden crates. When we pulled the tarp off of them, we found that they looked just like those we had seen in the mine. The only difference was that they appeared to have been opened.

We moved over to the crates and I shined my light inside. At first glance, both crates appeared to be empty. I wondered what had been in them. Could it have been treasure pirated from others on the Great Lakes?

"I don't think these crates have been here very long," I whispered. "Most of the dust and dirt has been knocked off them from being recently moved and opened, but there are still some cobwebs on them."

Monica stepped up and shined her light into one of the crates as I shined my flashlight down at the floor. I was looking for tracks from a two-wheel cart, which I quickly found. The tracks were the same as the ones in the mine and confirmed my belief that the crates had recently been moved into the basement from the mine.

"Look at this," Monica whispered.

I turned around to find her reaching into one of the crates. When she pulled out her hand, she was holding a small gold broach. Holding it in the open palm of her hand, she turned her flashlight on it to examine it more closely. I moved up beside her and looked at it.

"That looks very old," I whispered.

"I would guess that it dates back, maybe a hundred years or possibly a little more. It's hard to tell. But I can tell you that it is from England," she said.

I looked at her and smiled. This woman never ceased to amaze me.

She looked up at me and smiled back.

"It's my job at the university. I identify these types of things all the time, but I usually have better light to do it in," she whispered.

"Look here," I whispered as I pointed my flashlight toward the floor. "There are the tracks from a two wheel cart. I think it's the same one that was used in the mine. The wheel tread looks the same. My guess is someone brought these crates in here from the mine to empty them and then carry off whatever was in them."

"Where would they put what was in the crates? These crates are pretty big," Monica asked.

She had a way of asking the most interesting questions. I had to take a minute to think about it before I could come up with a way.

"My best guess is they empty one or two of the crates a night, loading what is in them into their cars. Those big Lincoln Town Cars sitting out front have pretty big trunks. Then they probably take it somewhere safe, like a storage locker. Somewhere where they can repack it without being seen. Then they ship it to wherever they want. At least, that's how I would get it moved."

Monica seemed to agree with me and returned to looking around the basement for any more jewelry that might have been dropped.

I began following the tracks across the floor. They led to a door that was made of oak, but this door didn't appear to be as heavy as the door I had seen in the mine.

After examining the door, I tried the handle. I found it to be unlocked. I carefully released the latch and slowly pulled open the door.

When the door was about half way open, it began to squeak. I froze in my tracks and held my breath as I listened. Neither of us moved as we looked up toward the ceiling and listened for any sound that would indicate that someone might have heard the noise. I held my breath as I waited and listened.

I was hoping that the squeaking of the door did not alert anyone that we were down here. At the same time, I was trying to decide if we should get out of the basement before we were discovered, or if we should continue our search.

"What do you think? You think anyone heard that?" Monica asked in a whisper as she looked toward me.

"I don't know."

"I sure hope not," Monica replied, her concern showing on her face.

I shined my flashlight around behind the door as I squeezed through the opening. Inside was a narrow tunnel. I shined my flashlight down the tunnel. At the end of the tunnel was another door. I glanced down at the floor and saw the tracks of the two-wheel cart. I noticed that the floor of the tunnel was pitched downward, which meant that each step along the tunnel would take us deeper below the surface.

I started down the tunnel with Monica following close behind. We moved quietly down the tunnel toward what I was sure would be the door into the icehouse. The tunnel was only about fifty feet long, yet in that fifty feet it must have dropped down about eight to ten feet deeper, maybe more. We could feel the air getting colder as we got closer to the door.

We came up to a large heavy oak plank door. At first I thought we might be on the other side of the door we had seen in the mine, but as I looked at it, I could see it was different.

I carefully checked out the door. For one thing, it was not appear to be as heavy a door as the one in the mine. It also had newer, more modern hinges and latch, and they looked like they had been changed recently. There was a hasp on the door, but no lock. However, there was a large bolt that secured the door. I slid back the bolt and tried to open the door. It wouldn't budge.

"Hold this," I said as I handed Monica my flashlight.

I got a good grip on the handle of the door and put my shoulder against the door and pushed as hard as I could. Suddenly, the door gave way and I almost fell through the door.

As the door opened I thought I heard a whooshing sound like that of a sudden rush of air. It was then that I realized that there was a slight breeze coming from inside.

"There's such a draft on this door that it almost wouldn't open," I whispered.

"I heard kind of a whistling noise when you opened the door," Monica said.

I didn't think the sound would carry very far as it was not very loud, but I still stopped to listen for any other sounds. When I didn't hear anything, I reached out to Monica for my flashlight. She handed me the flashlight, and I shined it into the room.

I slowly moved into the room with Monica following close behind me. There was no doubt that it was the icehouse. Along one wall were several boxes of frozen foods. Hanging from an overhead beam was a side of beef wrapped in cheesecloth and frozen solid. There were other boxes in the room that looked like they really didn't need to be frozen. It appeared that the icehouse was used as a storage room as well as a freezer. Although it was not quite as cold as a modern freezer, it was still cold enough to keep things frozen.

"I can see why they call this an icehouse. It's very cold in here," Monica whispered.

Suddenly, we heard the door close behind us. At first I thought it was just the draft causing it to close, but that thought quickly vanished when we heard the distinct sound of that large heavy dead bolt being fastened on the other side of the door.

I ran to the door and pulled hard against it, but it wouldn't open. The realization that we were locked in came quickly, along with the realization that someone was going to use the icehouse to kill us.

"You are right, my dear. It is very cold in there," a voice from the other side said in a hushed whisper.

Monica grabbed my arm and held me tightly. I knew she was frightened, and I couldn't blame her. The thought of freezing to death was not a pleasant thought at all.

"It won't do you any good to scream, my dear, no one will hear you," the voice informed us.

The voice was somehow familiar, yet it wasn't. It sounded a little bit like Andrew Thorndike, but in a whisper it was hard to tell. It could have been Elinor Mortimer, but there was no way for me to be sure. There was no doubt in my mind that either of them was capable of locking us in the icehouse to freeze to death without giving it a second thought.

"We'll be missed, you know that. Someone will come looking for us," I insisted. "So you might as well let us out, now."

"Oh, I couldn't do that. Just so you know, by the time anyone would think to even look for you down here, we will not only be gone, but you will be in no condition to tell the authorities anything. Have a pleasant night."

Monica was about to say something, but I put my hand over her mouth and motioned for her to be quiet. She looked at me as if I was crazy, but she seemed to trust me enough not to make a sound.

I listened carefully as the sound of the footsteps slowly faded away and disappeared. When I heard the faint sound of the door at the other end of the tunnel close and the latch catch, I turned to Monica.

"We'll get out," I reassured her calmly.

"How?"

"Through the mine," I whispered softly.

"What if that door is locked from the other side?"

"It won't be."

"What makes you so sure?"

I could hear a hint of panic as her fear of freezing to death began to take hold of her. I needed to calm her and reassure her that everything was going to be all right.

"Remember the door in the mine? There's no lock or latch on the other side. The door only latches from this side. Whoever shut us in here doesn't know that we have been in the mine. They don't know that we have a way out."

Monica looked at me as if she was trying to understand what it was that I was telling her. She moved up to me and leaned against me. I wrapped my arms around her and held her close. By holding her, I may have been reassuring her, but I was not so sure that we could get out of here. We were not dressed for any real long stay in such a cold place as this. Our jackets were too light, we had no gloves and it was extremely cold and damp.

We hadn't had much time to look around, but I had not seen the door that opened into the mine. It had to be around here somewhere. Maybe, it was behind those shelves, or possibly behind the crates stacked along one of the walls. There was no time to waste trying to guess where the door might be, it was time to start looking for it.

"Honey, we have to find a way out of here," I whispered. "You take that side of the room and work from the door to the middle of that wall," I said as I pointed to the wall opposite of the door we had entered. "I'll start on the other side."

Monica immediately stepped away from me and started looking for the door. We looked behind all the boxes and shelves for the door. I was beginning to think that there wasn't any door. Maybe the door we had seen in the mine went some place else.

It wasn't until I got to one corner of the large room that I found the door that we were looking for. It was carefully hidden behind several large crates that were very heavy and had been stacked all the way to the ceiling.

"I found it," I said and waited for Monica to join me.

As she stood behind me, I shined my flashlight along the wall between the large crates. We could just barely see the very edge of the door. I then stepped back and shined my flashlight over the crates in an effort to figure out how we were going to move those large heavy wooden boxes.

"We'll never be able to move those heavy crates," Monica said with a discouraged tone in her voice.

"I'm sure whoever shut us in here was counting on that, but there is a way to that door, there has to be one."

"What makes you so sure?"

"They brought the loaded crates in here from the mine and took the empty boxes back out to the mine. They had to move these crates to do that. If they can move them, so can we," I said as I looked over the crates.

I stepped up to the crates and pushed against them. They didn't budge, not even a little. I pushed on them again, only harder this time, nothing.

"They're frozen together, and to the floor. We'll never be able to move them," she sighed.

Maybe, she was right. One thing was for sure, the crates were solid. Suddenly it came to me. That was it. They were just a little too solid for crates that were simply stacked against a wall. Crates of that size should have moved at least a little when I put my full weight against them. They had to be hooked together somehow.

I again stepped back to get a better look at our problem. There had to be a way to move those crates, after all they had been moved before. Someone had to move them to get Mrs. Thorndike into the crate in the mine without being seen.

Then I remembered something. Where was the two-wheel cart? I hadn't seen it in the icehouse. I shined my flashlight on the floor. It took me a minute, but I found the tracks and they led right under the center crates. We had been trying to move the crates along the edge, when all we had to do was to open the crates in the middle.

I moved back up to the crates in the center. I began looking and feeling around the edges of the crates for some kind of latch, hinge, or something that would give me a clue as to how they opened.

"What are you doing?" Monica asked.

"You are right, these boxes are solid, too solid. I think they were built here to hide the door. There has to be a way to open them," I replied as I continued to search for a way to get them to open.

Monica hesitated for a few seconds and then she joined me in the search. Suddenly, one of the crates sort of popped open, just a little. She had accidentally touched one of the crates in just the right spot to release the catch.

"Look!" she cried with excitement.

"What did you do to get it to open?"

"I don't know. All I did was push about here," she said as she pushed on another crate, which immediately opened.

I reached over and pulled the crates wide open and found that the insides of the crates formed a small open area, almost like a closet or a place to hide. The crates formed a false wall that was used to conceal the door to the mine.

Monica quickly followed me inside, then I closed the crates behind us. I quickly opened the door that led into the mine. As soon as Monica was in the mine, I made sure that the crates were closed tightly before closing the door to the mine behind us. We quickly made our way to the entrance of the mine and stepped outside into the warmer night air.

CHAPTER FIFTEEN

As we hurried out of the mine, the warm night air rushed over us as if we were being covered with a warm blanket. It felt good after being in the icehouse and the cold mine. Knowing that it was only a short distance from the mine to the lodge, I quickly shut off my flashlight to avoid anyone accidentally seeing the light.

Monica was shaking so badly that I had to take the flashlight from her and shut it off. I then wrapped my arms around her and held her close. She was still shivering and I was sure that most of it was caused by the fact that someone had tried to kill us.

"You okay?" I asked as I rubbed her shoulders to help get her circulation going again and to release some of the tension.

"No," she said as she looked up at me. "I've never had anyone try to kill me before."

The look on her face in the moonlight told me that she couldn't understand how anyone could kill another person, especially by leaving them in the cold to freeze to death.

"You're safe now," I assured her.

"I don't feel very safe," she said in a soft sigh.

I didn't feel very safe, either. I needed time to think.

"Now what do we do?" she asked.

Even in the moonlight I could see the concerned look in her eyes. Her eyes were pleading for an answer, but I didn't have any answers for her. I needed time to think before answering.

I looked around. The moon was only about three-quarters full. Although it gave us some light, it wasn't enough that we could see our way through the woods without the use of our flashlights. We had to be careful not to shine them so that they could be seen from the lodge. If we put our fingers over the lens of the flashlight we could get enough light to see our way, but not enough that it could be seen from the lodge.

"I don't know," I finally replied.

"We can't go back to the lodge."

"We have to go back to the lodge. Whoever is involved with all this is about to pack it in and leave. Once they're gone from here they will be harder to capture."

"Just who are 'they'?" she asked, the tone of her voice showing that she was frustrated.

"I'm not sure who all is involved. Until we have some kind of proof, we won't know for sure. There is one thing in our favor, though."

"And what is that?" she asked. The tone of Monica's voice indicated that she could not think of anything that could even remotely be considered in our favor.

"Whoever they are, they think that we are locked away where we will freeze to death before we are found," I explained.

"And how is that an advantage to us?"

"Thinking that we are out of the way, they will feel safer and just might take a little more time to do what they planned."

"That will give us a little more time, too," she said as she began to think about it.

"Right. We need to go back to the lodge so I can talk to Tom."

"Are you sure that's a good idea?"

"Why? You still think that Tom might be involved?"

"I don't know, but if he is, then we will have told him everything."

I didn't like what she was getting at, but on the other hand, she just might be right. I couldn't take the chance. It would be better if we kept what little we knew to ourselves, at least for now.

"Honey, did you keep that broach?"

"Yes. I have it in my pocket," she replied as she took it out of her pocket and held it out to me.

"I thought that it might come in handy if we have to try to prove what is going on here," she added as I took it from her.

That gave me an idea, but I was suddenly interrupted by the sound of a sports car's engine starting. The only one I knew of who had a sports car at the lodge was Monica. I didn't wait for a response from her. I quickly let go of her and ran through the woods toward the lodge.

Just as I got to the edge of the woods, I saw Monica's sports car being driven away. It had no more than disappeared from sight when Monica came up beside me.

"What's happening?" she asked as she looked past me toward the lodge.

"Looks like they had this pretty well planned out. Someone just drove off in your car."

"My car!" she said excitedly.

"Shhhhhhh. I think it was Thorndike."

"Why would he steal my car?" she asked in a whisper. "Wouldn't that just add to their problems?"

"I doubt it. Think about it. For the past couple of days we have used your car to go everywhere while my car has set out in front of the lodge."

"I see. If my car's not parked out in front but yours is, everyone would think that we've gone off somewhere together. It would look normal to the other guests," she added in a whisper.

"Right. And if the others buy that, then no one will miss us."

"That also means that no one will be looking for us. That will give them all the time they need to finish up and leave," Monica said.

"True, but it might also give us sometime. If they think we are out of the way and will not be missed, then they might not be in such a hurry to get away," I reminded her.

"Look, its Thorndike," she whispered as she pointed toward the lodge.

"He couldn't have taken your car very far. I'll bet it's probably hidden just off the side of the road."

"Are we going to go looking for it?" she asked.

"Yes, as soon as he is back inside the lodge. When we find it, we're going into town."

We waited until Thorndike had time to get inside the lodge before we moved. I took Monica by the hand and walked to the edge of the woods. After checking to be sure there was no one else around, we began walking along the edge of the road staying in the dark shadows as much as possible.

As soon as we were out of sight of the lodge, we began walking down the road. Monica walked along one side of the road while I walked along the other. We were looking for someplace where a car could be driven off the road and hidden out of sight that was not very far from the lodge.

We had gone only a short distance when I noticed some mud on the side the road. Putting my fingers over the front of the flashlight so it gave off only a little light, I shined the flashlight on the mud. I could see fresh tire tracks in the mud. I shined the light on the tracks and then followed them until they disappeared over a little knoll between some trees.

"Over here," I called to her quietly.

Monica crossed the road to see what I had found. After showing her the tracks, we followed them up over the knoll. We immediately found her car not more than twenty feet off the road on the other side of the knoll.

I did a quick visual check of the car to make sure that nothing had been tampered with, and that it was still drivable. I didn't find anything wrong with it. It looked like it had simply been driven out here and left, which seemed to make sense. After all, Thorndike was probably convinced that no one would be looking for it, and we were the last people he would expect to drive away with it.

"Looks okay to me," I said.

"Are the keys in it?" she asked.

I shined my light into it and discovered that the keys were not in the ignition. I turned and looked at her, hoping that she had a set in her pocket.

"No keys. Do you have a set with you?"

"No. You told me not to carry anything in my pockets that might rattle. I left my keys in my room. He must have taken them from my room."

I looked at the car, then back at her.

"I guess I'll just have to hot-wire it."

She stepped back away from the car while I opened the door, bent down and looked under the dash. It took me a few minutes to find the right wires, but as soon as I did and crossed them the car started.

"You're almost too good at this. Did you steal cars as a kid?" Monica asked with a grin.

"No, but a friend of mine taught me how."

"I take it he was good at it."

"Not really. He's in jail for stealing cars. Now get in and let's get out of here," I suggested.

She got in and I carefully backed the car out onto the road, being as quiet as possible. Being so close to the lodge, I didn't want anyone to hear the car. After easing the car out onto the highway, I let the car slowly pick up speed as we drove away from the lodge. When I was sure that the car could not be heard back at the lodge, I let it out and we sped along the highway toward town.

I began to think and consider our options. It would be well after four in the morning before we could get to Sturgeon Bay. I doubted that there would be anyone on duty at the Sheriff's Office that would take us seriously at that hour. Another thought occurred to me, what if Mrs. Thorndike's body had been removed from the mine. In that case, we would be looked at as if we were nuts. Our credibility with the police would certainly be lost.

I also began to think that we just might be headed in the wrong direction. If we turned around and went back to the lodge, and I could get into Arthur Mortimer's room, I might be able to get him to talk to me. If I could get him to talk, then we might have a chance of convincing the sheriff that a crime was committed and who committed it.

It was going to do us little good to notify the sheriff at this point. If the body had been removed from the mine, and we didn't have someone else to support our story, we would have no proof. The only thing the police would do would be to go to the lodge and question everyone. That would simply alert the killers and give them the chance to escape, and that was the last thing I wanted to happen.

"We're going back to the lodge," I said as I slammed on the brakes and turned the car around in the middle of the highway. We were headed back toward the lodge before Monica had a chance to say anything.

"Are you crazy?"

"I sure as hell hope not."

"Well, I'm not so sure. They have already tried to kill us once."

"As I see it, we don't have enough evidence to go to the police. We have to have more proof, enough proof to get them arrested so they can't escape. And if there is one thing that I know, it is that you have to have some kind of proof that a crime was committed before anything will be done."

"Like what? What do you think you can find that would provide proof?"

"Arthur Mortimer," I replied.

"Mortimer?"

"Yes. Did you see the look on his face when his wife escorted him away from the table?"

"Yes, - - - sure," she said as she began to think on the same wavelength that I was on. "He was scared to death of his own wife. Do you think he knew that Thorndike and his wife had already killed Mrs. Thorndike?"

"I don't know, but he is one very frightened man. He just might be scared enough to talk to us. If we can get to him, he just might open up and talk."

"He might not, too," she said.

"That's true, but it's a chance I believe we have to take."

She certainly had a point there. If he didn't talk, it could ruin everything for us.

"How are you going to get to him without his wife knowing?" Monica asked.

"That part I don't know. I think we will have to get to Tom, first. Maybe, he can help."

"Are you sure that's a good idea?"

"No, but it's the only idea I've got. Do you have a better one?"

"No," she admitted.

Reluctantly Monica agreed, at least she didn't say anything more about it. I still had my doubts about Tom, but I had to trust my instincts. When I got to the place where the car had been hidden earlier, I pulled off the road and parked it in the same spot. At least if they came to check on it, it would still be there.

We worked our way through the woods to the back of the lodge. I slowly looked over the lodge for any signs of life. The only lights that were on were the lights that Tom always left on. All the rooms appeared to be dark, and the lodge appeared to be quiet.

Staying in the shadows as much as possible, we worked our way to the back door. I carefully pulled the screen door open, then slowly turned the knob and opened the door. We entered the lodge.

Off to the left, I noticed a narrow staircase. I hadn't remembered seeing it from the second floor. I took the flashlight from my pocket and shined it up the dark stairs.

"Do you remember seeing this staircase from the second floor?" I asked Monica in a whisper.

"No. Where do you think it goes?"

"I'll bet this goes up to the third floor, directly to Tom's apartment."

"You want to try it?" Monica asked.

"Might as well. You got a better idea?"

"No," Monica replied.

I covered part of the lens of my flashlight so it would give off just enough light for us to be able to see the steps. Slowly, we started up the steps being careful not to make any unnecessary noise. If my estimates were correct, the staircase passed right between the newlywed's room and Mortimer's rooms.

At the top of the stairs, we came to a door. Looking back down, I was sure that we had come far enough to have passed the second floor of the lodge. I was sure that we were on the third level. It was obviously the private staircase to Tom's apartment.

I looked at Monica and she looked at me. I could see she was holding her breath as she waited for me to try the door. Slowly turning the knob, I was a little surprised to find that the door was unlocked and that it opened easily. As we stepped through the door, a quick look around told me that we must be in the small kitchenette of Tom's apartment.

"Now what?" Monica whispered as she reached out and took hold of my arm.

"We find Tom," I replied softly.

Following me as closely as she dared, we began wandering through the apartment. It didn't take us long to find Tom's bedroom. I motioned for Monica to wait at the door while I went inside the bedroom. As I moved quietly up to his bed, he rolled over on his side, which caused me to stop in my tracks and hold my breath.

As soon as he settled down again, I moved up along side the bed. I carefully reached down and quickly covered his mouth, which caused him to immediately wake up. My touching him like that scared him and his eyes flew open, but he did not try to roll away. As soon as he realized who it was, he seemed to relax and looked at me as if I had gone crazy.

"Don't say a word," I whispered. "Do you understand?"

He nodded that he understood so I took my hand from his mouth. I sat down on the edge of the bed as he sat up.

"What the hell is going on? You scared the hell out of me," he whispered.

"Keep your voice down. We don't want anyone to know we're here," I whispered. "I'm sure I did, but I need some information."

"Damn, Nick, it's the middle of the night."

"Look, I don't have time to explain everything to you now. Let it suffice to say that someone tried to kill us tonight."

"Kill you!"

"Yes. Now listen. We want to know what room Arthur Mortimer is sleeping in?"

"Why?"

"Just tell me, Tom. I don't have all night."

"He's in the room across the hall from you, room six."

"What room is Mrs. Mortimer in?" Monica asked.

"She is in room four, right next to six."

"Are they adjoining rooms?" I asked.

"No. They asked for separate rooms when they checked in."

"Who is in room three, next to mine?" I figured that I might as well know where everyone should be.

"Andrew Thorndike and his wife. Mr. Beresford is in the room next to them. The newlyweds are in room two on the other side of the hall. There is no one in room eight," Tom explained.

"Good. Does room eight have an adjoining door to room six?"

"No. You and Miss Barnhart have the only adjoining rooms."

"Tom, I want the key to room six. I need to get into that room tonight."

"Sure, but why?"

"We think that Arthur Mortimer knows the answers to some very important questions. We want those answers, and it can't wait."

Tom looked at me as if I had gone over the edge, but he reached over to the bedside table and picked up a ring of keys. He picked out one key, took it off the ring and handed it to me.

"That is the master key to all the rooms on the second floor," he explained.

I looked over at Monica and then back at Tom. The thought that she might be right about Tom gave me reason to pause. I didn't like taking unnecessary chances, but I couldn't bring myself to believe that Tom would be a part of any of this, at least not willingly. I also couldn't take the chance that he wasn't a part of what was going on, either.

"I'm going to go pay Mr. Mortimer a visit. I'll be back shortly. You stay here and keep quiet. Don't even walk around," I instructed Tom.

Monica took my hand as I started to go by her. I stopped and gently squeezed her hand.

"Be careful," she whispered.

"You, too," I said as I looked back over my shoulder at Tom.

I gave her a light kiss on the cheek, then went to the apartment's front door. I opened the door as quietly as possible, stepped out onto the landing and shut the door behind me. I took a deep breath before I started down the steps.

CHAPTER SIXTEEN

The stairway down to the second floor was lit only by a single small night light about half way down the stairs. It cast a glow over the stairs that gave me just enough light to make out the steps. I slowly worked my way down the stairs staying as close to the edges of the steps as possible in order to avoid causing any of the steps to squeak. Once at the bottom of the stairs, I turned and started down the hall, stopping only briefly at each door to listen. All was quiet.

When I reached the door to room six, I stopped and stared at the doorknob. I had only my hunch to guide me, no clear-cut facts to tell me what to do. If I made a wrong choice, the whole thing could blow up in my face and I could easily end up sitting in jail while the killers escaped. Worse would be if Tom was a part of it, and he had set me up by giving me the wrong key.

As I hesitated, I looked down at the key in my hand. It was clear that our only hope in getting the whole thing solved was to get Arthur Mortimer to talk to me. I was sure in my own mind that he knew what was going on, who was involved, and who had actually killed Mrs. Thorndike.

The time had come to do what I was sure needed to be done, or turn around and go back to Monica. It was a clear choice, either try for the proof I needed to end all this, or go to the police with what I knew and with what little proof I had to back it up.

Going to the police without sufficient proof could jeopardize our chances of catching the killers of Mrs. Thorndike. I had to try to prevent their escape from justice.

Then, I remembered something that Tom had said, room eight was empty. As I thought about the placement of the other guests in the lodge from the information Tom had provided and from what I already knew, I was convinced that Tom's information had been correct, at least about room eight.

I took a quick look at the door to room six then moved on down the hall to room eight. If it was empty, it would give me a good chance to find out if the key I got from Tom really worked without waking anyone. I carefully slipped the key into the lock. With only a slight clicking noise, the door unlocked. I turned the knob, slowly opened the door and peered inside.

There was light shining in the window from a yard light outside. I could see that the room was empty and quickly stepped inside the room, silently closing the door behind me. So far, Tom's information had been correct.

Taking the flashlight out of my pocket, I turned it on to get a better look around the room. The first thing I noticed was a door in what I was sure should have been the wall between rooms eight and six. Tom had told me that there were no adjoining doors between the rooms. If he was telling me the truth, then the door would be a closet door. If not, then there was a good chance that I had been set up and he was a part of what was going on here.

I examined the door carefully. It didn't have a lock in it. The adjoining room doors between Monica's room and mine had locks. I took hold of the doorknob and slowly turned it. The door opened into a rather shallow closet. I suddenly felt as if I could breathe with a little more confidence now.

The closet was empty. I closed the closet door and looked around the room some more. Over in the corner, at about a forty-five degree angle to the walls, was another door. I thought it was strange to have a door in the corner of a room like that, a door that couldn't possibly go anywhere.

Then it hit me. That door could very well lead into the tower on this end of the lodge. I walked across the room and tried the door, it was locked. I tried the key that Tom had given me, but it didn't fit. Checking the door very closely, it appeared to be a different kind of lock than I had seen on the other doors in the lodge. From the looks of the scratches on the door, the lock had been changed very recently.

It occurred to me that somebody didn't want anyone going into the tower. I wondered who that someone might be. I knew that Tom didn't want anyone in the tower, but my gut feeling told me that there was also someone else who didn't want anyone in the tower, but for a completely different reason than Tom's.

Whatever was in the tower would have to wait until another time. Right now, I was more interested in what Arthur Mortimer might know. I left the room and returned to the hallway. I stopped at the door to my room. I took hold of the doorknob and quietly set the door ajar.

Checking once again to make sure that the hall was clear and everything was quiet, I returned to the door of Arthur Mortimer's room. I put my ear up against the door and listened. I could hear nothing. I hesitated for a second when the thought that this might be a setup passed through my mind again. Taking a deep breath, I carefully slipped the passkey into the lock. The key turned easily. Slowly and carefully, I turned the doorknob and pushed the door open. The room was dark accept for a little light that filtered in along the edges of the window shades.

"Who is it?" asked the soft shaky voice of a frighten man.

"It's me, Mr. Mortimer, Nick McCord. Don't be frightened, please. I just want to talk to you for a minute," I whispered.

"Please, get out," he whispered. "If my wife catches me talking to you, she'll kill us both."

I had to agree with his assessment of the situation. It was clear that he had a good understanding of his wife. I had to say something to calm him before he raised his voice and woke his wife or Andrew Thorndike. It was apparent that he was scared of both of them, and it was that fear which had kept him quiet. It was that very fear that I would use to get him to talk to me if I couldn't get his cooperation any other way.

"Please, Mr. Mortimer. I want you to come across the hall to my room. I need to talk to you. I wouldn't have disturbed you if it wasn't extremely important."

"I can't. If I do anything Elinor doesn't like, she will beat me," he whispered.

"Mr. Mortimer, if you don't come with me now, you will be talking to the police. I don't think that Elinor will like that very much, either."

I felt I had little or no choice. I had to know what he knew. If I had to threaten him to get him to talk, then so be it.

I could tell by the way he looked at me that he was mulling over what I had said in his mind. I hoped that he was more afraid of talking to the police than he was of coming with me. The longer I stayed in his room, the greater the chance I stood of getting caught with him, and that would not be good for either of us.

Finally, he sat up on the edge of the bed. He took his robe from the chair next to the bed and slipped his arms into it as he stood up. I went to the door and slowly opened it. After checking the hall and finding it clear, I hustled Mr. Mortimer across the hall to my room. Once inside my room, I felt a little more secure about dealing with him.

"Arthur, do you know what is going on here?"

He didn't answer my question, but simply stared at me. I had a feeling that it was going to be very difficult to get any information out of him. I could not remember ever seeing a man so afraid of his own wife.

"Arthur, you're going to have to talk to me or to the police. Take a look at that picture," I said as I pointed to the picture of Elizabeth Samuelson. "That is the woman that was found in the ice on the beach. What can you tell me about her?"

Arthur looked at the picture for what seemed like a very long time. It was as if he was trying to decide just how much he should say. He then turned and looked at me.

"Elinor is related to that woman by marriage. The Thorndikes are from Bartholomew Samuelson's mother's side of the family. The Thorndikes are, and have always been mean, nasty and greedy people, especially the women. Bartholomew's mother was supposed to have killed her husband because he tried to leave her for another woman," he explained.

"Andrew Thorndike and your wife are brother and sister, aren't they?"

"Yes," he answered quietly as if he were ashamed of it.

"Why are they here?"

He looked at me, but didn't answer. From the look in his eyes, I was sure that he knew more than he was willing to say, but was afraid to answer any more questions.

"Okay, you don't want to talk to me. How about if I tell you a few things?

"First of all, your wife and her brother devised a plan to frighten Tom Walker in an effort to drive him out of the lodge. Their plan failed, so they produced a dead body that they were sure would keep people from coming here, causing Tom to lose money and eventually forcing him to sell the place. That plan was going along pretty smoothly until Miss Barnhart and I showed up. We just happened to show up on the same day.

"Mrs. Thorndike got scared that I might figure out what was going on and they would get caught. She told your wife about her fear of getting caught. To prevent her from possibly spilling the beans, your wife killed her and put her body in the icehouse."

I intentionally didn't say anything about the mine. I didn't want to reveal all my cards. He didn't even flinch when I mentioned the killing of Mrs. Thorndike. I was sure that he knew about it, but I doubted that he had taken any kind of an active part in it.

"You know that if you had any part in the killing of Mrs. Thorndike, or know who did it and didn't report it, that you could be held as an accessory?"

"I don't know anything. Please let me go back to my room before my wife finds me gone," he pleaded.

It was clear that I wasn't going to get anything more out of him tonight. He was too afraid to talk to me. I guess I couldn't blame him for that, after all, I would not be able to protect him from his wife and he knew it.

"Okay. If you change your mind just let me know."

I stood up and led Arthur to the door. After checking the hall and finding it clear, I let Arthur leave and return to his room.

I had failed to get his cooperation, but worse than that I had let him know that I was still alive and well. He would more than likely be able to figure out that Monica was also still alive. If he told his wife about my late night visit with him, neither Monica nor I would be safe. I had to return to Tom's apartment and get Monica out of here, and fast.

I waited in my room until I was sure that Arthur had time to return to his bed. When I was sure that the hallway was clear, I left my room and went down the hall to the stairs that led back to Tom's apartment.

When I arrived back at Tom's apartment, I found Monica sitting in a chair across the room from Tom. Tom just looked at me as I walked up next to Monica.

"How did it go?" Monica asked in a whisper.

"Not well. I'm afraid that I may have let the cat out of the bag. Mortimer is too afraid of his wife to even talk to us, and now he knows that we are still alive."

"Do you think he will tell the others?" Monica asked.

"Maybe, but only if he figures it will keep him from harm."

"What do we do now?"

"I don't know, but we are going to have to do something pretty soon. If Mortimer talks, things will end here rather quickly."

"I have an idea," Monica suggested, but stopped short of saying anything more.

I got the message loud and clear. She was not willing to say anything more in front of Tom. A quick glance at Tom made me think twice, too. I don't know what it was, but he seemed to be just a little too alert to what we were saying for a man who was supposed to be scared out of his mind.

"Tom, I'll keep in touch. We have to leave now, but we'll be back."

"Okay, but don't be gone too long. I'm afraid of those people."

I looked into his eyes. For the first time, I was not sure if he was telling me the truth. I had been going along with Monica up until now, but there was something about the way he looked at me that convinced me that Monica just might be right about him.

We turned to leave Tom's apartment. We had our backs to Tom as we started toward the door. Monica casually directed my attention to a small gold pin lying on a circular table near the door. The pin looked to be rather old and very valuable to me, but I was not the expert on such things.

As soon as we got to the door and Monica had stepped through the doorway, I turned around to face Tom. He had followed us to the door.

"I will be in touch with you tomorrow," I said.

"When?" he asked.

It was a simple enough question. If it had been asked by anyone else, I wouldn't have thought twice about it. But Tom asked it, and I have never known Tom to be the least bit concerned about time. Maybe I was becoming a little paranoid, but at this point I found it difficult to trust anyone.

"I don't know, but I'll be in touch."

He appeared to be disappointed that I would not tell him exactly when I would be contacting him. That was just one more reason for me to be suspicious of him.

As I turned to leave, I took Monica by the arm and we started back down the stairs. We wasted no time in getting out of the lodge. I had this overwhelming feeling that it was not safe for either of us to be in the lodge.

We returned to Monica's car as quickly as possible and got in. I was about to start it, but hesitated. I looked over toward her.

"What's the matter?" she asked.

"Do you think that pin on the table is part of the treasure?"

"I can't say for sure. I didn't get a very good look at it, but it could be. It looked like it was old enough."

"Damn!" I said wishing that it was not true.

"You think he's involved, don't you?"

"I didn't. Do you?"

"I'm still not sure. I just wanted you to be cautious until you were sure one way or the other."

"Well, I'm not sure, either," I said. "If he is not involved with the others, then I think he knows more about the lodge than he has been letting on."

"If he is not involved with the others, then what is he up to?" Monica asked.

"There are three possibilities. One, he is involved with what is going on up to his neck. Two, he is not involved with anyone else and he is trying to find the treasure himself.

Three, things are just what he has said they were and he is afraid for his life," I explained.

"What about the gold pin?" Monica asked.

"It would be my guess that he either found it by accident, or he has found some of the treasure."

"What do we do now?" Monica asked.

"We need to find us a safe place to get some rest."

"It's a little late to get a motel room around here."

"I wasn't thinking of a motel. If we check into a motel around here, they would know it before the sun comes up."

"There's that old cabin near the entrance to the mine. It's not much, but we have a blanket in the trunk and it would provide us some shelter," she suggested.

"Good idea," I said as I reached down and started the car.

We drove to a place as close to the mine as we could get and walked the rest of the way to the cabin. The cabin was nestled back in the trees and was only about fifty yards from the mine entrance. It would provide us with shelter and allow us a chance to get some much needed rest without worry of being easily found.

I entered the cabin first with Monica right behind me. It was clear that the cabin had not been used for many years. There were cobwebs in the windows and in the corners. The floor looked as if it had not been swept for years, which it probably hadn't. It was run down, but it was a roof over our heads and a place where we were not likely to be found.

We spread the blanket down on the floor. All I can say is that it was a good thing that it was a warm night. If it had been a cool night, one blanket would not have been enough.

I stretched out on the floor and Monica lay down beside me. She curled up against me, resting her head on my shoulder. I knew it wouldn't be long before the sun would come up. It was important that we get some badly needed rest. Tomorrow could turn out to be a very busy day.

I found it hard to get to sleep as my mind was going over all the things that had happened in the past few days. I had solved many other puzzles, but at this moment I could not remember one that was so confusing and so complicated. My biggest problem was that I had no idea where all of this was leading.

I could feel Monica as she snuggled up closer to me. She had already fallen asleep. I tried to close my mind as well as my eyes, but it took me a long time before I finally drifted off into a deep sleep.

CHAPTER SEVENTEEN

I woke up suddenly to the sound of a creaking noise coming from outside of the cabin. It sounded like someone or something was moving slowly along the porch close to the wall. I could even follow the movements as it moved toward the cabin door.

As I turned and looked toward the door, Monica sat up and looked down at me. I motioned for her not to make a sound then I rolled over and stood up.

I took a quick look around the cabin for something that I could use as a weapon to defend us and ward off any intruders. There was an old wooden table leg lying near the fireplace. I moved across the room as quietly as possible and picked it up. I then moved over close to the door.

The sound on the porch was getting closer and closer to the door. I gripped the table leg in one hand as I glanced over at Monica. As I looked back at the door, I carefully reached out and took hold of the doorknob. I readied myself to open the door.

Another glance at Monica made it clear that she was frightened. It was now or never. I mentally counted to three then quickly jerked the door open. I was posed and ready to do battle in defense of our lives only to discover that I had just scared the hell out of some poor old raccoon that scurried away as fast as his short little legs could carry him.

I must have looked like Don Quixote standing there holding a table leg over my head ready to smash the brains in of my enemy, in this case a fat raccoon. I let out a sigh of relief as I turned around and looked at Monica. She had her hands over her face as she tried not to laugh at me. I grinned, but it was more a release of my fears and nervousness than the fact that it was so funny.

Monica smiled at me and said, "My hero."

I couldn't help but to laugh. I set the table leg up against the wall next to the door. I went back to our blanket on the floor and sat down beside her. She reached out and took hold of my hand. Her hand felt warm and soft. It took me a few minutes to get my nerves to settle down. It had been a raccoon this time, but who knows what it might be next time.

As I sat down on the edge of the blanket next to Monica, my mind returned to the problems that we faced. There was a lot running through my mind, much of it not very pleasant.

"I was thinking," I said as I turned toward Monica. "When whoever it was who locked us in the icehouse returns to get the rest of the treasure in those crates and we are not there, they are going to know that we know about the mine," I said thoughtfully.

"Won't they figure that we escaped out the door they locked?"

"I hope not," I replied as an idea came to me.

I could tell by the look on Monica's face that she was beginning to think that I had gone totally crazy this time. A broad smile came over her face as she began to realize that I had thought of something really sneaky.

"I should know that you are planning something devious. What's going on in your head?" she asked.

"Suppose, just suppose, that when they come back tonight to get the rest of the treasure from the mine; and not only are we not there, but the treasure is not there, either" I said as I looked at Monica for a reaction.

"God, it would drive them out of their minds," she said as she began to understand.

"Right," I replied.

"Okay, what do we have to do?"

The soft smile on Monica's face suddenly began to fade before I could begin to tell her about my plan. It was clear that she had thought of something that I might have overlooked.

"What is it?"

"Suppose that Arthur Mortimer, or Tom let's it be known to the others that we are not still locked in the icehouse. What happens then?" she asked.

After giving her question a moment of consideration, I replied. "It's too late to change what has already been done. We'll just have to hope that they don't say anything to anyone else, at least until we have removed the treasure.

"It's entirely possible that Arthur doesn't know we were locked in the icehouse, and let's hope that Tom is as quiet at the breakfast table as he has been up to now," I added.

Monica nodded as if she understood and agreed with my assessment of the situation.

"I think the first thing we need to do is to get something to eat. I'm starving," I said with a smile in an effort to ease her mind.

"Shouldn't we get started on moving the treasure out of the mine?"

"I don't think there's any hurry. They believe that they have us out of the way. They won't be able to remove any more of the treasure until tonight. With so many people around to see them, they wouldn't dare try to remove anything from the basement during the day."

"Won't we be taking the risk of being seen if we drive into town?" she asked.

"Yes, but we have a lot of work to do. If we don't eat, it could turn out to be a very long day."

"I suppose you're right. So, what's first?"

"If I remember correctly, there's a small convenience store in Ellison Bay about five or six miles down the road.

We can drive down there, pick up what we need and come back here."

"Okay," she replied.

I rolled up the blanket and set it on a shelf near the door of the cabin. As soon as we were ready, we walked back to where we had left the car and drove to Ellison Bay. When we arrived at the small convenience store next to the highway, we parked the car around behind the building, out of sight from the highway. We went inside and bought enough food to last us for at least two days.

While I was looking around in the store, I found a couple of backpacks that we could use to help carry some of the treasure out of the mine. I purchased the packs and a claw hammer to make it easier to open the crates. I also purchased some extra flashlight batteries, as I was sure that ours were just about worn out.

As we started out the front door, I grabbed Monica by the arm and quickly pulled her back into the store. I wasn't sure, but the big Lincoln Town Car parked out in front by the gas pumps looked very much like the one owned by Arthur Mortimer.

"Look there," I said as I pointed at the car.

"Is that Mortimer's car?" Monica asked.

"I'm not sure, but it looks like the one that was parked out in front of the lodge. If it is, where are they? I didn't see anyone come in."

I backed away from the door and led Monica around behind a display rack, then carefully scanned the room. It was going to be very difficult to hide in such a small store.

"Thanks a lot, Henry. I appreciate you getting this for me," a voice said.

I quickly realized that it was a voice that was not familiar to me. I looked out around the display and saw a rather tall man as he walked out of the store and got into the

Lincoln. I let out a sigh of relief and could hear Monica breathing a little easier, too.

"Let's get out of here," she said softly.

I couldn't agree with her more, but there was one thing more that I needed to do. I returned to the front counter of the store to speak to the storeowner.

"Excuse me, but I need a little information," I said.

"How can I help you?" he replied pleasantly.

"Does a Sheriff's deputy stop by here very often?"

The storeowner looked at me as if he were confused by my question, but answered me anyway.

"Yes. He usually stops by just before we close, that would be around seven-thirty, eight o'clock."

"If I don't come back here by the time he comes by tomorrow, would you ask him to contact Tom Walker at the Gill's Point lodge?"

"Sure," he replied.

It was clear to me that he wanted to ask me what it was all about, but his manners seemed to prevent him doing so. I watched him as he scribbled a note to remind himself.

"You might ask him to question Tom Walker about where I might be," I instructed the owner, then gave him my name.

The storeowner looked up at me and then quickly added that information to the note. He had a strange look on his face as I turned and led Monica out of the store and around to the back.

"What was that all about?" she asked as we put our supplies in the car.

"I figure that we are going to need some help. When they discover that all the treasure has been removed from the mine, they are going to come unglued. There is no telling what will happen then."

"But what good will it do us tomorrow night? We will probably need the help tonight."

"With human nature like it is, I suspect that he will tell the deputy tonight about it. The deputy will have a hard time waiting and might show up early, like late tonight or early tomorrow morning. At least this way, if my plans fall through someone will know about us.

"There's also another thing. Police officers are inquisitive people. Thinking that something might happen in a certain area tends to keep the officers in that area," I said.

Monica seemed to understand what I was telling her, but the look on her face gave me the impression that she was still worried about our safety. I couldn't blame her for that, I didn't have any idea what Elinor and Andrew might do. It was clear to me that they would not hesitate to kill anyone who got in their way.

I started the car and drove out from behind the store. I was careful to look for any signs of someone from the lodge that might see us. Turning the car out onto the highway, I sped toward the road that would take us back into the woods.

Monica did not say anything as we watched the road. I wasn't sure what she had on her mind, but I was wondering where all this was going to lead. The more I thought about it, the more I began to realize just how much danger I had put her in. Even though it had not been my intention, I had done it just the same.

"I'm sorry," I said disturbing her thoughts.

"What? Sorry about what?"

"I'm sorry that I dragged you into this mess."

She looked at me. A smile slowly came over her face as she reached out and put a hand on my leg.

"I'm not," she replied softly.

"It could get a little sticky."

"I know, but I can't think of any place else that I would rather be right now."

I glanced over at her, then turned back to watch the road. I had to wonder if she might regret those words by this time tomorrow.

It was not long before we reached the turn off into the woods. I stopped the car, got out and looked both ways down the highway.

"Drive the car out of sight," I told her.

Monica got behind the wheel and drove the car down the dirt road until it could not be seen from the highway. I found a branch with a lot of leaves on it and began to brush our tracks out of the dirt. When I reached the car, I throw the branch off to the side and got back in the car.

We drove to where we had been hiding the car. After gathering up our supplies, we walked back through the woods to the cabin.

It was almost mid-morning by the time we sat down on the rickety old porch of the cabin to eat our breakfast. We had a long day ahead of us. If we were to succeed in getting all of the treasure out of the mine before dark, we were going to have to get started soon.

"I know that you want to get all of the treasure out of the mine today, but what are we going to do with it? Where are we going to hide it?" Monica asked.

"In that cave we found yesterday."

"Isn't that pretty close to the mine? They might find it."

"Yes, it's close to the mine, but it's the perfect place to hide it. Its close, meaning we won't have to haul it very far. They would never expect us to keep it so close to where we got it. Plus the cave is well hidden and will not be easy for them to find."

A smile came over her face as she said, "You are sneaky."

"I know. I got you alone out in the woods with me, didn't I?"

"Yes you did, but I didn't know I was going to be moving crates of jewelry for you," she said with a slight chuckle in her voice.

"Speaking of that, I think we better get started."

She nodded her head in agreement as I finished my small bottle of juice. I stood up and held out my hand to her. She took hold of my hand and I pulled her to her feet. I gave her a light kiss before we picked up the packs and our flashlights and started toward the mine.

Once inside the mine, we made a quick check to see if anyone had been in the mine, or was possibly still in the mine. There was no one, nor were there any signs that anyone had been had in the mine since last night. I opened the first crate I came to and let Monica start loading the contents into her pack while I opened another crate.

The crates contained all kinds of valuable items from gold coins to personal items. The first crate contained mostly jewelry, which appeared to be well over a hundred years old. The other crates contained some jewelry along with sterling silver cups, serving sets, plates and goblets. In one crate, I even found some crystal glassware. Another crate was full of gold cups, plates and gold coins. The value of all these things was almost unbelievable.

We took trip after trip of valuables from the mine and carefully hid them in the cave. Much of the valuables were very heavy and it was not long before we needed to take a break. We found a place just outside the mine entrance where we could relax for a moment or two. Monica flopped down on the log and I sagged down beside her.

"What time is it?" she asked.

"About twelve-thirty, why?"

"It seems that we have been working longer than that, is all," she answered with a sigh.

I was just about to say something to her when I heard voices off toward the lodge. I knew we were close to the lodge, but I didn't think we would be able to hear anyone at the lodge. I could not make out what was being said, but I was sure that it was a man and a woman talking.

I motioned for Monica to get down and be quiet. I pointed toward some bushes for her to hide behind. I was not sure if they were coming our way.

As soon as Monica was out of sight, I carefully worked my way toward the voices. I moved slowly so I would not be seen or heard. When I got to a place where I could look up over the ridge and see who was on the other side, I crouched down behind a log.

Just a few feet inside the woods from the lodge's lawn, I saw Elinor Mortimer and Andrew Thorndike. Elinor seemed to be very upset with Andrew, but I couldn't tell why. I worked my way up a little closer until I was sure that I was as close as I could get without being seen.

"Damn it, Andrew, what the hell did you do that for. They couldn't prove anything."

"It didn't matter if they could prove anything or not. All they had to do was mention what was going on and the police would be all over the place. They were slowing down progress. Besides, I don't know what you have to complain about, you killed Priscilla," Andrew said.

"Keep your voice down. I had to kill her. She was about to talk. We couldn't have her spoiling the whole thing for us. I don't know why you brought that woman along, anyway," Elinor complained as she shook her head in disgust.

"How would it have looked if I had come here alone? I needed a wife and she was available," he replied angrily.

"Well, it's too late now. I figure that we have three days, no more than four, before we have to be out of here. If we play our cards right, we will have everything out that is of any value," Elinor said.

"I can keep up the pretext that my wife is not feeling well for a couple more days, but not much longer. The others will get suspicious," Andrew assured her.

"Arthur is getting nervous, too, but I can keep him quiet."

"Make sure you do. He could cause us a lot of problems if he decides to talk," Andrew complained.

I watched them as they turned and walked back toward the lodge. It was clear to me that I had come in on their conversation when they were talking about Monica and me. At least now I was sure who was involved, and who had locked us in the icehouse.

As soon as it was safe, I turned and worked my way back away from the ridge making sure that I was not seen. Monica came out from behind the bush when I returned.

"Who was it?" she asked.

"Elinor Mortimer and Andrew Thorndike. I'm sure it was Andrew that shut us in the icehouse."

"Did he kill Mrs. Thorndike?"

"No. Elinor did."

"What do we do now?"

"We need to finish what we've started, then I think we should get some rest. We're going to pay another visit to the lodge tonight," I said as I took Monica by the hand and led her back toward the mine entrance.

I was sure that Monica was thinking that this was getting out of hand and could get worse, but she didn't say anything. The worried look on her lovely face faded away as we walked back toward the mine entrance. It was quickly replaced by a smile. I leaned down and kissed her lightly on the lips. When we got back to the mine, we went inside to finish what we had started.

We spent most of the afternoon removing more of the treasure from the mine. It was hard work, but we finished just shortly before five. The only things left in the mine were a bunch of empty crates, neatly closed and made to look as if they had not been touched. The only crate that we left undisturbed in the mine was the one that contained the body of Priscilla.

CHAPTER EIGHTEEN

It had been a lot of hard work, but we had removed all the remaining treasure from the mine to the small cave. After we made sure that we had left no tracks behind that would lead anyone to the cave, we worked our way back to the cabin. Feeling the stress of the day, I sat down on the porch. I leaned back against one of the posts and let out a sigh of relief. Monica sat down beside me and leaned up against my shoulder.

We had spent a lot of energy getting the treasure out of the mine and into the cave. It was rather warm outside the mine and I was feeling sweaty and dirty. I needed a bath and a change of clothes, but it was not safe to return to the lodge, at least not until late tonight.

"I wish we could get a bath and a change of clothes," Monica said as if reading my mind.

"I was thinking the same thing."

"How about if we go for a swim? It would at least help rinse off some of the sweat and dirt," she suggested.

"Sounds good to me, but we can't risk being seen," I reminded her.

Monica looked disappointed, but she soon had another suggestion.

"If we went through the woods until we were, say, - - far enough down the beach that we could not be seen from the lodge, would that be okay? We could take a quick dip in the lake with our clothes on. At least that would be better then nothing," she quickly added in her effort to get me to agree.

I had to admit that her idea sounded very appealing. A quick dip in the cool water to rinse off our bodies and our clothes would feel good about now. It was certainly warm enough that our clothes would dry in a very short time.

This woman was something else. She could talk me into almost anything, plus the fact that she did have a good point.

"Okay, but we have to go at least far enough to be out of sight of the lodge. We have to be very careful not to be seen by anyone. We have no idea who might be involved in this," I reminded her again.

She smiled at me, then leaned over and gave me a light kiss on the cheek. She was one woman who was not only smart, she was beautiful.

"I'll get our blanket," she said as she stood up.

I watched her as she went into the cabin. My mind began to fill with thoughts of what might happen once Elinor Mortimer and Andrew Thorndike discovered that the rest of the treasure was gone. There was no doubt in my mind that they were in for one hell of a surprise, a surprise that would most likely turn to anger and eventually turn to violence. It was also clear to me that they could be as cold and calculating as any killer I had ever dealt with, and I had dealt with my share of them over the years.

My head kept telling me that if I really had any feelings for Monica, I would get her out of here and back to the University where she would be safe. The longer this game of hide and seek went on, the more dangerous it would become. And the longer it went on, the greater the chance that Monica could get hurt or even killed.

I resolved to get her out of here as soon as possible and finish what we had started alone. It would be much easier for me if I knew she was safe.

"You ready?" she said interrupting my thoughts.

"Ahh - - yes. Yes, I'm ready," I replied looking up at her and forcing myself to smile.

"What's wrong?"

"Nothing," I said, but I got the distinct impression that she might not have believed me.

I stood up, reached out and took her hand. We walked through the woods in the direction of where we had left her car. When we got to the dirt road, we turned and walked in the direction that was away from to the highway. We walked until we came to the narrow beach at the end of the road.

Before walking out of the woods onto the beach, I carefully checked out the area to make sure that there was no one around who might be enjoying the sun, sand and water. There was no one, but I didn't like it right here at the end of the road. I felt that there was too much of a chance that someone might just come down the dirt road to the beach for a swim and see us. I couldn't take the chance.

"It looks clear enough, but I would rather go down the beach just a little further."

We walked out of the woods and took another look around. I could see quite a way up the beach toward the lodge, but I could not see the lodge from here nor could I see anyone on the beach.

"What about down there?" Monica asked as she pointed toward a small inlet just a little further down the beach.

"I wouldn't think the water would be very deep there. It might even be a little warmer than out in the lake," she added.

The spot that she had picked out was also very near the trees making it easier to slip back into the woods without being seen if someone should come along. It looked like a nice secluded place. I had to agree with her assessment. After our last swim in the lake, I wouldn't mind at all if we found a place where the water was a little warmer.

"Looks good to me," I replied.

She took me by the hand and together we walked down the beach toward the inlet. I made it a point of checking behind us often to make sure no one had come out onto the beach.

As we approached the water, we stopped just long enough to drop the blanket, remove our shoes and for me to put my wallet and keys in them. Fully clothed, we walked into the water. It got deep rather quickly, deeper than I had expected. I had to admit that the cool water was refreshing as it soaked through my clothes and I stepped out into deeper water.

Although the water was cool, it was much warmer than out in the lake. I bent at the knees and let myself go under the water, rinsing some of the sweat and dirt from my face and hair.

When I surfaced, I glanced over at Monica. She was standing in water that was about waist deep. She had obviously been under water, too. The sun sparkled in her soft, wet, blond hair, and the look on her face showed a feeling of refreshment.

As she tipped her head back, she reached up and pushed her hair back away from her face. Her wet clothes clung to her lovely body, accenting the smooth lines of her figure and the firm round shape of her breasts. A smile came to her face as she saw me looking at her.

I waded over to her. As I approached her, I reached out and took hold of her waist. She wrapped her arms around my neck and drew me to her. She tipped her head back and closed her eyes as our lips met in a long passionate kiss.

The feel of her body and the warmth of her lips quickly shut out the rest of the world for me. She let out a soft moan and pressed her lips harder against mine when I pulled her shirt loose from her jeans. Our kiss continued as I pulled her wet shirt up her body. She let go of me and raised her arms up while I pulled her wet shirt up over her head, exposing her bare breasts to the warm sunshine. She then pulled her arms free of the shirt.

Resting her hands on my shoulders and looking up into my eyes, she suggested, "We could wash out our clothes and hang them on a tree to dry."

I continued to look into those deep blue eyes of hers as I gently slid my hand up and down the smooth skin of her sides while I thought about her suggestion. At that moment I could not think of a single reason to object.

"Okay," I replied in a hushed whisper.

"I'll lay out the blanket over by the trees. Since you already have my shirt, you can start washing out our clothes."

I smiled as she gave me a quick kiss on the lips. She then let go of me. I watched her as she waded out of the water toward the blanket. Droplets of water on the smooth skin of her back sparkled in the sun. After she disappeared into the woods, I realized that I still had her shirt in my hand. I rinsed out her shirt first.

Monica returned just as I was taking off my shirt. I rinsed my shirt out while she stood at the edge of the water and removed the rest of her clothing. I handed her our shirts and watched her as she again disappeared into the woods.

It was hard for me to keep my eyes off her as she moved with the grace and smoothness of a professional model. The smooth flowing lines of her body, the gentle sway of her hips and the way she carried herself as she moved away from me made it impossible not to watch her. She was a very sexy lady. I couldn't see what she could see in me.

As soon as she was out of sight again, I took off the rest of my clothes and quickly rinsed them out. When I was finished, I waded out of the water and walked back into the woods where she was hanging up our clothes. Just inside the woods, I saw her as she was arranging the last piece of clothing over a tree branch to dry. She took part of the clothes I had and hung them up on the tree while I hung the rest.

"Now we can rinse ourselves off," she said with a smile.

I reached out and took her hand in mine. We walked back to the inlet and into the water. After we had rinsed the sweat off, she waded up to me. Slipping her arms around my neck, she drew herself up against me. I wrapped my arms around her and held her tightly. The warmth of her naked body was a pleasant contrast to the cool water.

She tipped her head back and closed her eyes as I leaned down until our lips met. It was a long passionate kiss that sent a warming sensation through my entire body. Her skin felt soft and cool under my hands as I gently slid them up and down her back.

We broke off the kiss and she leaned back slightly looking up into my eyes as I looked down at her. I could still feel the warmth of her firm breasts pressing against my chest, but it was the soft deep blue of her eyes and the smooth porcelain appearance of her face framed in wet, golden blond hair that brought me to my senses. I could not help but think that with every hour that passed, I was placing this beautiful woman in danger.

"What's the matter?" she asked softly.

She must have sensed what I was thinking. The softness of her eyes seemed to become darker as if she had suddenly realized that I was not totally engrossed in her as I should be under the circumstances. Instead I was thinking about something else.

"Nothing," I replied.

This didn't seem to be the right time or the place to discuss it. I was hoping for a better time, a time when there was nothing else to think about.

"You're not playing fair," she said as she ran her fingers through the hair on the back of my head.

"I'm not?" I asked as I playfully slid my hands down over her firm butt, gently squeezing her.

"No, you're not. You may be holding me in your arms and touching me with your hands, but your mind is on something else. You mind letting me in on it?" she asked, the expression on her face turning very serious.

I thought for a minute before answering her.

"I'm worried about you," I admitted.

"That's sweet," she replied with a smile.

"You don't understand."

"What don't I understand?"

"When Elinor and Andrew find out all the treasure is gone and the fact that we are not dead in the icehouse, they will be looking for us. We will be the targets for their anger."

"What are you saying?" Monica asked.

Although she asked me to explain, I had a feeling that she already was beginning to get my message.

"I'm saying that if they find us, they will do whatever it takes to kill us."

Monica looked into my eyes for a couple of seconds before she spoke.

"You want me to go away. You want me to go someplace where I will be safe, don't you?" she said as she put her hands against my chest and pushed backed away from me.

"As a matter of fact, yes. I'd be lying if I said otherwise. I'm a cop. I'm used to this sort of thing. You are not," I said in an effort to make her understand.

She looked at me as if I had smacked her across the face. I could see the fire in her eyes and the anger on her face. Her whole body seemed to radiate her anger and frustration with me.

I knew that she wouldn't want to leave, but I had not expected such determination on her part to see it through to the end. Before I could respond, she turned her back to me and waded out of the water. I stood there, sorry that I had said anything as I watched her disappear into the woods.

It hit me hard. I suddenly realized that she needed to see it through with me, and I needed her to be with me. I had to do something to let her know how I was feeling. I had to let her know that I really did want her with me.

I ran out of the water and quickly followed her into the woods. When I got to where she had laid out the blanket, I found her sitting on it with her legs tucked up and her arms wrapped around her knees.

When she glanced up at me, I could not miss the sad, hurt look in her eyes. She quickly looked away, trying to keep me from seeing the tears in her eyes. It made me feel like a heel. After all, she had helped me from the beginning and now I was telling her that she could not be there for the end.

"I'm sorry," I said softly as I knelt down beside her.

She refused to turn and look at me, and I couldn't blame her. I reached out and touched her arm. She finally turned her head and looked at me.

"I'm sorry. I'm just worried about your safety. I care very much about you. Is that so hard to understand?"

"No," she said softly. "I'm worried about you, too, but I'm not asking you to run and hide."

"Point well taken, I'm sorry," I replied softly.

I had to agree with her. Without her help, I wouldn't have as much information about the history of the lodge, and I wouldn't know as much about Elinor Mortimer and Andrew Thorndike. It would not be fair to prevent her from seeing it through.

She started to lean toward me and I toward her when we heard voices coming from near the beach. I motioned for her to remain quiet while I slipped off the blanket and moved toward the sound of the voices. When I was several feet away from the blanket, I looked back and signaled for

Monica to get dressed, and to bring me my pants. I continued to move closer to the edge of the woods.

From where I was hiding at the edge of the woods, I could see thirty to forty feet in both directions. Up the beach toward the lodge, I could see Elinor Mortimer and Andrew Thorndike. They appeared to have been having a rather heated discussion. Neither one of them were talking at the moment. It was impossible to tell what they had been talking about.

"Here," Monica said in a soft whisper.

I turned around to find her kneeling behind me and holding out my pants. She moved up next to me and looked out toward the beach while I slipped into my pants.

"What's going on?"

"I don't know. I can't tell from here. I'm going to try to work my way up closer."

As I started to turn, she reached out and touched my arm. I stopped and looked into her eyes.

"Be careful," she whispered.

I winked and gave her a slight smile, then turned and started working my way up along the edge of the wood. The mixture of sand, dried branches and leaves made it hard to move very fast and still remain unnoticed. When I got about as close as I could without being seen or heard, I settled down behind a dead tree and listened. Andrew looked at Elinor. He seemed disgusted with her.

"Are you sure that Miss Weatherspoon will not be missed?" Andrew asked.

"Of course I'm sure. I would not have let you bring that woman along if I thought for one minute anyone would miss her, or that anyone around here would know her. No one will miss a prostitute, especially here," Elinor replied. "All you have to do is keep up the story about your wife not feeling well for two more days."

Andrew seemed to be concerned about the woman he had been passing off as his wife as if he really did have some feelings for her. I had had a feeling that she was not his wife, but now I knew that I had been right. Miss Weatherspoon was just some poor woman who got involved with Thorndike, then got in over her head. She knew too much, and they disposed of her like a sack of garbage.

"Have we walked far enough?" Elinor said with a hint of anger in her voice. "We need to get back to the lodge. We have a lot of work to do tonight."

"What about Arthur?"

"What about him?"

"I'm getting worried about him. If he talks to anyone, we'll be finished."

"He won't talk to a soul. I increased his medication. He doesn't have the faintest idea what's going on," Elinor replied. "I doubt that he even knows where he is anymore. Now can we go back?"

"Yes," Andrew replied.

I watched them for a few more minutes as they turned and started back toward the lodge. I had to wonder what type of drug they were using on Arthur that kept him so frightened and timid. It made me wonder what he had been like before he was put on the drug.

As soon as they were out of sight, I returned to Monica and told her what was going on. Tonight would have to be the night if we were going to get the answers we needed.

After I told Monica about the part of their conversation that I had heard, we finished dressing and rolled up our blanket. I only wished that I had been able to hear all of their conversation. I had to wonder what I had missed. If I had heard it all, we might have some idea of what to expect. As it was, we were just guessing and that makes it dangerous.

We arrived back at the cabin only a short time before dark. We ate our dinner of cold sandwiches and juice in silence.

After we finished our meal, I sat back on the porch and leaned against the cabin wall. Monica laid down and rested her head on my lap. We didn't talk as I ran my fingers lightly through her soft hair. I sat quietly while we waited for the darkness of night.

CHAPTER NINETEEN

The darkness of night came slowly to the cabin even though it was nestled deep in the woods. The air was beginning to slowly turn cooler. A gentle breeze drifted in off the lake carrying with it the soft sounds of the night.

There was the faint rhythmic sound of the waves in the distance as they gently splashed against the sandy shore, and the constant clicking sound of crickets around the cabin. I could also hear the sounds of pots and pans clanking together as the cook and his helper cleaned up after the evening meal at the lodge.

As I sat on the porch of the cabin with Monica's head resting in my lap, I thought about this night and what we were planning to do. It was a time to worry. I was worried that things might not work out quite like I had hoped. If that should happen, it could mean that someone might get hurt or even killed.

There was no doubt in my mind about the danger that lies ahead for us. We had done something that would anger those we had set out to find. What made it really dangerous was that we were not sure of everyone that might be involved.

My thoughts once again returned to Monica and her safety. I had to question whether or not I had done the right thing when I decided to let Monica stay to the end. Would it not be better to lose her from my life and know that she was safe, than to risk her life?

My fear for her safety was making me wish that I had been more forceful in insisting that she be someplace else. But the more I thought about it, the more I realized that I really had little to say about it. She had made the choice to stay with me and see it through to the end. I had tried to get her to go back to the University where she would be safe, but she definitely had a mind of her own. It was actually one of the things that made me like her.

Just then I felt her stir and looked down to see her looking up at me. I smiled, but I must have failed to hide my concern for her safety from my face.

"I know you're worried about me, but don't be," she said softly as she reached up and put her hand lightly against my cheek. "Everything will work out."

"And if it doesn't?" I retorted softly.

"Then don't blame yourself," she said. "I chose to stay. I insisted on staying until the end. You certainly didn't force me to come with you."

What she said was certainly true. However, it did nothing to relieve my concerns, nor did it help me keep from worrying about her.

I ran my fingers lightly through her soft hair. It was dark and I could not see the deep blue of her eyes, but I knew that she was looking up at me and hoping that I would understand why she had to stay with me.

She slid her hand around behind my neck and gently pulled me down toward her. I leaned over until our lips met in a soft gentle kiss, a kiss meant to tell me that she needed to be with me tonight, no matter what happened.

I pulled back slightly, still looking at her beautiful face in the dim moonlight.

"It won't be long, now," I said softly. "The house will be dark soon."

I could feel the tension as well as the excitement in her, or maybe it was more the tension and excitement in myself that I was feeling. It made me alert to every sound, every touch and every movement around me. It had been a long time since I had felt the adrenaline in my body fill my senses and awaken every nerve in my body to my surroundings.

I could feel the heat from her body, as she lay curled up beside me with her head in my lap. It was almost as if I could feel her heart beat along with mine. She moved her hand and I immediately felt the movement. The touch of her hand on mine was almost like a spark of electricity going through me.

I looked at the soft glow of her face as she took my hand, placed it gently over one of her breasts and held my hand to her. I could feel the warmth of her breast as well as the firmness of it in the palm of my hand. I could also feel her heartbeat. She moaned softly as she gently guided my hand over her breast.

"I like to have you touch me," she said in a hushed whisper.

Touching her like this took my mind off what was to come, at least for a few brief moments. But the thought of the possible danger to her by returning to the lodge quickly brought me back to reality.

"It's time we start our plan," I said as I removed my hand from her breast.

Reluctantly, I helped her sit up beside me. As she sat up, she leaned over and gave me a quick kiss on the cheek. I wanted to say something romantic, but my mind was too filled with the risks tonight would bring. We were going to confront one or more killers. Not being sure of all who were a part of it, only made it that much more dangerous. This was no time for me to be distracted.

"We know that Elinor, and probably Andrew, killed Mrs. Thorndike, or should I say Miss Weatherspoon. We know that they are taking the treasure of Captain Samuelson from the house and hiding it somewhere, possibly in a storage locker somewhere nearby.

"We also know that they have been frightening Tom with noises and visions, and we have even figured out why," I said as I reviewed what we seemed to know so far.

"It sounds as if we have it all together. Now all we have to do is call in the police and let them sort it all out," she added with a note of confidence.

"Not quite."

"What's left?" she asked, the look on her face showing that she couldn't understand what else was needed.

She hesitated for a second, then added, "I understand what you are saying, that we need proof. But don't you think that once the police find the body of Miss Weatherspoon that they could wrap this up without the two of us getting any more involved?"

"Possibly," I conceded. "But I don't want whoever else is included in this to get away because we bring in the police too soon."

"I don't understand. Who else besides Elinor and Andrew is involved?"

"That I don't know, but think of this. We are dealing with a rather bizarre case here, in which I continue to get the feeling that someone other than the relatives of Elizabeth and Bartholomew Samuelson are involved."

"Who? The only ones who are not related to Elizabeth or Bartholomew are Tom, you and me."

"And possibly the newlyweds," I added.

"Do you think that they are involved? You have been saying all along that you don't think they're a part of it," she asked confused by my comments.

"I still don't," I reaffirmed.

"Then the only one left is Tom, unless you think that I'm involved somehow."

"You and I are the only ones that I am sure about. It's Tom that has me confused," I confessed.

Monica looked rather surprised that I had come to the conclusion that Tom might be involved. I could see by the look on her face that she did not understand my thinking and how I had come to that deduction. I wasn't sure myself why

I was beginning to feel that Tom might be involved right up to his neck.

I tried to think of what it was that was sticking in the back of my mind that kept directing me toward Tom. Maybe it was the broach Monica found in Tom's room. Maybe it was his concern for when I would return. Or maybe it was the fact that he didn't tell me about the connection between the icehouse and the mine. Whatever the reason that I felt the way I did, I sure hoped that I was wrong.

If he was involved, just how was he involved? It was possible that he was mixed up with Elinor and Andrew, but something in the back of my mind told me that was not the case.

I already knew that Elinor had killed Miss Weatherspoon, but what did Tom have to do with it? This whole damn thing was getting more confusing. The more I thought I knew, the more I was unsure of what I knew. It seemed as if my mind was cluttered with way to many unknowns.

My thoughts were interrupted when Monica reached over and touched my hand. She seemed to sense how much it disturbed me to think that one of my longtime and best friends might be involved in murder, but then maybe he wasn't. Maybe his involvement was only in removing part of the treasure. Yet, I knew that if he was involved with Elinor and Andrew, he would be considered an accomplice to murder. Then again, maybe he wasn't involved at all. I could hope that was the case.

"I'm sorry," she said softly. "I wish I hadn't said anything that would make you question Tom's friendship."

"It's all right. If it hadn't been for you wondering about him, I might have put us in much more danger by trusting him completely. At least this way, I will be watching him more closely and hopefully not be caught off guard by him should he be involved. If he isn't involved, then there will be no harm done," I said more in an effort to reassure myself then anything else.

I kept trying to tell myself that Tom couldn't be mixed up in any of this, but I couldn't help but feel that there was a chance, however slight, that he might be. The only thing that I needed to figure out was just how, and to what degree he was involved.

Time passed slowly as we waited for the lodge to get quiet. The sky was clear and full of brightly shining stars. The moon was not full, but it still gave off a good deal of light. I could hear an owl hoot in a nearby tree and then the flutter of its large wings as it flew away. It seemed strange that such a quiet night could easily turn into a night of violence.

I glanced over at Monica and wondered what she was thinking about as she sat looking out into the darkness. I wondered if she was trying to search her mind for answers to the same questions I had, or if she was possibly thinking about us.

She was beautiful with the soft glow of the moonlight on her face and on the smooth strands of her blond hair. To see her looking so peaceful was a stark contrast to how I was feeling.

"Are you sure you won't go into town and wait for me," I said softly, hoping that she might concede and get away from here before it got to dangerous.

She quickly turned and looked at me. The look on her face made me almost wish I had not said anything.

"I'm sorry," I apologized, but I had to try one more time to get her to change her mind.

A soft smile came over her face. I was sure she understood my concern for her safety. She leaned toward me and I toward her until our lips met. It was a light kiss that I was sure was meant to reassure me of her commitment to being with me tonight.

"Don't you think it's about time," she said as she pulled back a little and looked into my eyes.

"Yes," I replied as I let go of her.

We stood up and went inside the cabin. After checking the flashlights inside the cabin so no one would see them, we were ready.

Leaving the cabin, I took her hand in mine and we worked our way to the edge of the woods. We crouched down behind some bushes and looked out over the area in order to make sure that all was quiet.

After I looked from window to window to make sure that all the lights were off that should be, I motioned for Monica to follow me. I quickly moved across the lawn to the back porch with Monica close behind. We kept to the shadows as much as possible. I crouched down next to the porch and pulled her down next to me.

"Wait here," I whispered. "Don't make a sound, and don't move from here."

"Where are you going?" she asked softly as she grabbed my arm in an effort to stop me from leaving.

"I think a little support might be needed," I whispered. "I'll be back in a second."

I leaned over and gave her a light kiss on the forehead in an effort to reassure her that I knew what I was doing. I then turned and quickly moved along the lodge to the corner. I worked my way around to the front of the lodge and looked out at the cars parked in front.

My car was parked where I had left it, apparently undisturbed. I took a quick look around. Seeing no one, I ran over to my car. Ducking down behind it, I opened the trunk as quietly as possible and just far enough to be able to reach inside. It didn't take me but a second or two to find the locked box that I kept hidden under the old blanket.

From the locked box I removed my 9mm automatic and checked it to make sure it was loaded and ready to use.

After slipping it quickly into my belt, I closed the trunk as quietly as possible and returned to the back of the lodge where I had left Monica. I knelt down beside her.

"Where did you go?" she asked in a whisper.

"To my car," I answered in a whisper as I pulled open my jacket so she could see the gun.

"Do you think we need that?" she asked as she looked up at my face.

"I hope not, but it's nice to have just in case. Let's go."

We stood up and Monica followed me to the back door. I stepped up on the porch steps and slowly opened the screen door being as careful as possible not to make any noise. The door needed to be oiled and I hoped that no one had heard it squeak. I slipped inside the back porch with Monica right behind me. She followed me into the kitchen.

As I moved around past the cutting table in the middle of the kitchen, I accidentally brushed against something on the edge of the table and it fell to the floor with a crash. In the silence of the kitchen it sounded to me as if I had dropped a whole drawer of silverware on the floor. When in fact, it was a single spoon that I had knocked off the edge of the table.

We froze in our tracks with Monica holding my arm and standing beside me. I was sure that she was holding her breath as I was. We didn't move for what seemed like a half an hour, but it was more like a minute or two. We waited and listened in an effort to determine if anyone else had heard the noise.

We could hear no other sounds in the house. I let out a long breath as I began to breathe again. I glanced over my shoulder at Monica. She was just beginning to breathe again, too.

Again, I started to move through the kitchen to the dining room door, being just a little more careful that we didn't cause any more noise. Easing the door open, I peeked into the dining room.

The room was dimly lit by a small night light. There was enough light to see that no one was in the room. It looked as if the table had already been set for breakfast.

Monica followed me as we moved around the large table and across the room to the door to the main room. Standing next to the door with Monica right behind me, I looked over my shoulder at her to make sure she was all right. In the dim light I could not see the deep blue color of her eyes, but I could see the sparkle in them. I could even feel her breathing as she was standing so close to me.

I turned back around and looked at the door, then slowly pushed it open just a crack. The night lights in the main room cast an eerie glow over the entire room giving it the appearance of a haunted house. I could see why it would be so easy to create the elusion of a ghost in that room.

I slowly scanned the room trying to see if anything was different, even just slightly different. The first thing I noticed was that the fire had burned down and there was the soft glow of slow burning embers. The room was quiet, yet it invited one to come in and sit down.

As I continued to look about the room, my eyes caught something in the dim light. I tried very hard to understand what I thought I was seeing. Then it registered. The panel that led to the basement was ajar and the chair that usually sat in front of it had been moved to one side, out of the way.

I turned and looked over my shoulder and whispered to Monica, "Someone's in the basement. The panel is open."

"Any idea who?" she whispered in my ear.

"No, but I think we better find out," I said as I looked at my watch.

I pushed the dining room door open a little further and slipped into the main room keeping as much in the shadows as possible. Monica followed me through the door and along the wall to a dark corner where we were not likely to be seen.

"Now what?" she whispered.

"We wait and watch," I said as I placed a finger over my mouth as a reminder that we needed to remain very quiet.

Just then I heard sounds coming from the basement. Someone was coming up the steps from the basement. We stepped back deeper into the corner to wait and see who was coming out of the basement.

CHAPTER TWENTY

"I don't know why I let you talk me into this damn fool plan of yours. Nothing has gone right from the very start."

Although the male voice was hushed and low as he stepped out from under the stairs into the main room, the quietness of the room allowed us to hear every word he said clearly. The voice was that of a man who sounded as if he was very upset over something, and I was sure that it was because we had removed the rest of the treasure.

At this point I could not be certain who the man was, but my gut feeling told me that it was Andrew Thorndike. It wouldn't be long before we would know for sure.

"For the money, that's why." The voice of a female retorted angrily, but quietly.

We had another problem. In the dim light it was almost impossible to tell who these individuals were, although I was sure that I recognized the female voice as that of Elinor Mortimer. The bigger problem was we had no idea if they might be armed.

Silently, we slipped back further into the dark shadowy corner to watch and listen.

"This whole thing has gone downhill from the minute we got here," he said as he carefully closed the panel so it would not make any noise.

"It was your idea to bring that damn fool woman along, not mine," Elinor whispered as she returned the chair to its place in front of the panel.

"Maybe, but you didn't have to kill her," Andrew shot back.

"What should I have done, let her tell the world what we were doing?"

It was clear that Elinor was angry as she spoke through clenched teeth.

"What about that stunt you pulled with that woman's body in the ice on the beach. That was the dumbest thing I have ever seen you do. That brought the police down here and delayed everything for almost two months, valuable time was wasted, time that we needed," Andrew said angrily, but softly so that his voice would not carry.

"I told you I had nothing to do with that. I don't know who put that body there," Elinor rebutted.

I looked over toward Monica. Something about the way that Elinor said that she had nothing to do with the body in the ice convinced me that she just might be telling the truth. We had convinced ourselves that Elinor and Andrew had put Elizabeth's body on the beach in an effort to drive Tom either out of the lodge or crazy. We had not considered the possibility that someone else might have done it. The question now that remained was if they didn't put Elizabeth's body on the beach, who did?

Our eyes had adjusted to the dim light in the room as we watched Elinor and Andrew sit down in chairs near the panel to the basement. There was just enough light coming from one of the small night lights on the staircase that we could now see them clearly.

Andrew let out a long sigh, then said, "It's over and done with."

"What I want to know is where did all that treasure go? When we got here we found ten crates and they were all full. We emptied three of them worth about two hundred thousand dollars each. Yesterday, there were still six crates left with something in them, now they are empty, too. Do you think McCord and that girl might have taken what was left in the six crates?"

"Possibly," Andrew replied, but he didn't seem to be paying much attention to Elinor.

"You saw the mine, the crates were empty. Where the hell would they hide what was in them?" Elinor said thoughtfully, almost as if she was asking herself. "Back deeper in the mine, maybe?"

"There's just ice deeper in the mine, remember?" Andrew replied angrily. "We looked down deeper in the mine. There's nothing down there."

"One thing we never checked to see was if there was another way in or out of the mine. Maybe, they found a way out and took the treasure with them," Elinor suggested.

I watched Andrew as closely as possible in the dim light for some kind of reaction. He seemed to be contemplating something, maybe what Elinor had said. I was sure that he had little faith in her judgment at this point, but it was clear that he was thinking about something.

I was thinking about what had been said by Elinor. Where had the rest of the treasure gone? I had to wonder if Elinor had considered her own math. If we had the treasure from six crates, and they had the treasure for three crates, and if there had originally been ten crates, what happened to the treasure from the other crate? The only reasonable and logical deduction was that someone else had taken the treasure from the other crate.

What Andrew said next disturbed my thoughts.

"If those two got out of the icehouse and took the treasure with them, we could be in deep trouble. I wouldn't be surprised if they would go to the authorities," Andrew said thoughtfully as he slowly turned and looked at Elinor.

"Do you think they would be dumb enough go to the authorities when they certainly must know that the authorities would take the treasure away from them?" Elinor said with a disgusted look on her face. "I don't think so."

"You and I wouldn't, but I think that they might," Andrew said softly.

"I still don't understand how they could have gotten out of the icehouse," she said as if it were almost an afterthought. "The door was locked from the outside."

"What difference does it make how they got out, they got out. Did you see them frozen in the icehouse like they should have been?" Andrew asked angrily.

"No," she replied meekly.

"Did you see them in the mine?"

"No."

"Well then, where are they?"

"I don't know. They had to have found a way out," Elinor conceded.

"Right. If they weren't in the mine or the icehouse then they obviously found a way out and took the treasure with them," Andrew said with disgust.

My head was full of questions, too. We knew why the Mortimers and Thorndike had come here. It was to get the treasure from the icehouse and the mine. We knew that they had killed Miss Weatherspoon to keep her quiet and hid her body in one of the crates near the end of the tunnel. The question that still stuck in my head, that still remained unanswered, was who put Elizabeth Samuelson on the beach in the first place?

We knew from the conversation that Elinor and Andrew had at least a small portion of the treasure and that Monica and I had the major part of it. Although, I didn't really have much interest in the part of the treasure that seemed to be missing, I did have a great deal of interest in who might have it. If I could find out the answer to who had the missing treasure, I might be able to find out who put Elizabeth's body on the beach. I believed that the answer to that question would help me find out who it was that was trying to drive Tom out of the lodge. I figured that I already knew why they wanted Tom out of the way. The only remaining question was who?

"I think it would be a good idea if we got the hell out of here as fast as we can," Andrew said thoughtfully. "We should leave now."

"Tonight?" Elinor asked with a tone of surprise in her voice.

"Yes. Tonight," Andrew insisted.

"You want to leave all that gold and jewelry behind?" Elinor said angrily.

"What gold and jewelry?" Andrew shot back. "The rest of it is gone. We have been here for over three months and we don't have but, maybe, five or six hundred thousand dollars worth of old jewelry. All we've had is one delay after another. First it's the body on the beach and all those investigators all over the place. Then it's the ghosts in the main hall and more people nosing around, and now it's that McCord fella'."

"There was at least a million dollars or more in gold and treasure in that mine, it has to be somewhere. Someone has it," Elinor insisted.

"Sure. Someone has it, but who? McCord and that girl have some of it, you can bet on that. Another thing you can bet on is that we don't have time to hunt for it. We certainly don't have time to find out who has the rest.

"The longer we hang around here, the greater the chance that someone will find Priscilla's body. If that happens, the police could probably trace her death right back to us. I don't know about you, dear sister, but I do not wish to spend the rest of my life in an American prison," Andrew said with a bit of sarcasm in the tone of his voice.

We continued to watch them very closely. It was clear that Elinor was thinking over what Andrew had said. I was trying to decide just what to do when Elinor stood up and looked down at her brother.

"You're probably right, Andrew. We would be better off getting out of here with what little we have, than to risk staying here and possibly ending up spending time in prison. If we return to London, we might be able to get more for the jewelry because of its antique value than we can for the value of its precious metals and stones," she conceded.

It was time for me to make a move. There was no doubt in my mind that they were getting ready to pack it in and disappear. I couldn't let them get away.

Monica was standing next to me holding my arm tightly. Looking toward her, I motioned for her to stay back in the dark corner and not to make a sound. She nodded that she understood and let go of my arm. I stepped out of the shadows just as Andrew stood up. Reaching inside my jacket, I put my hand over my gun just in case, but kept it concealed from sight.

"Please excuse me for the interruption of this lovely family discussion, but I don't think you will be going back to London anytime soon," I said as I stepped into the light where they could see me.

Andrew turned suddenly to face me. From the look on his face, it was clear that he knew that I had heard everything that they had said. I had caught him off guard. It was also clear that he didn't know what to do about it. He simply stared at me as he tried to figure out what to do next.

I almost smiled at the surprised look on Elinor's face. She just stood there with her mouth hanging open and her eyes as big as teacups. She was frozen in place and didn't move one inch.

As the surprise seemed to wear off, Elinor's eyes once again showed the deep hate she had for me. I had to admit that her look could make me feel somewhat uncomfortable. It was like she was looking at me as if I was already a dead man.

"Now what, Mr. McCord?" Andrew finally asked as he began to regain his composure. "You think that you can arrest us? I certainly doubt that."

"Maybe, maybe not. But I do think the police will want to have a talk with the two of you. I've heard enough to see that you don't go back to merry old England for a good number of years, if ever," I said, sure that I had the upper hand.

"It would be your word against ours, Mr. McCord," Elinor said in a voice that seemed to be suddenly filled with too much confidence to suit me.

The tone of her voice matched the cold cutting stare of her eyes. I had met many women who were cold and ruthless in my life, but I could not remember ever meeting one as cold and as ruthless as this woman.

"You tend to forget one small matter," I said.

"And what might that be, Mr. McCord?" Elinor asked with polite sarcasm.

"There's the small matter of the body of one Miss Priscilla Weatherspoon, also known as Mrs. Andrew Thorndike to the rest of the guests at this lodge," I was happy to remind her.

"I don't believe that she will be found in her room upstairs resting comfortably as you, Andrew, have suggested at the dining room table. She will be found very dead and stuffed in a crate in the mine where you left her."

"Oh, really," Andrew added with a slight snicker in the corner of his lip.

The tone of his voice and the confident grin on his face gave me the distinct impression that he knew something that I didn't know. The first thing that crossed my mind was that they must have removed the body and hidden it somewhere else when they found out that we were not dead in the icehouse, but where? They had had plenty of time to remove the body from the mine before we got here, I thought. Without the body, I had the feeling that I would be standing on rather shaky ground with the local police.

"Where did you hide her?" I asked knowing full well that I was not likely to get an answer.

"Come now. You don't really expect me to answer that, do you?" Andrew asked, just a little too sure of himself.

"No, not really," I conceded.

"Well, we seem to be at a stand still, or a stand off as you Americans seem to prefer to call it. I don't believe that you will be able to prove anything," Andrew said with an evil grin.

"You might be right, Andy. You don't mind if I call you Andy, do you?"

"I most certainly do mind," he replied sharply.

"Well, Andy," I said with the intent of making him understand that I was not going to be intimidated so easily. "I think you are in a bit of a spot, as you Brits like to say. I know the two of you are guilty as sin of murder, and the theft of property from the lodge, but you are also right when you say I might not be able to prove it. But then again, I might.

"Since there seems to be nothing I can do to prove you guilty of anything right now, would you mind answering a simple question for me?"

Andrew glanced at Elinor and then he looked back at me.

"I guess I could do that much. What is it you wish to know?"

"How did you find out that there was hidden treasure here?"

Andrew glanced over at Elinor again as if he were expecting her to say something. She simply smiled at him and said nothing.

"It was very simple, really," Andrew said as he looked back at me. "Bartholomew Samuelson was, after all, a ship's captain. He was very much used to keeping a daily record of everything. One of his records was discovered hidden in the wall of his mother's home in Whinshire England when it was torn down about a year ago. Well, since I was the oldest known living relative, it was given to me.

"The pages were very difficult to read, faded and weathered, you know. It was originally thought to be the Captain's Log from his times at sea, or on your Great Lakes in this case. But I was able to discover that the journal was really of Captain Samuelson's activities as a pirate on the Great Lakes.

"The journal contained a fairly complete ledger of all the treasure that he had pirated from ships that were eventually reported as missing. With all he had taken over the years, he would have had to have some place very large to store that much. It was only a matter of deduction that brought me to the conclusion that his summer home on this out-of-the-way peninsula would have been the logical place for him to hide such a large amount of treasure," he explained.

"If you had all that information, why was it necessary to attempt to drive Tom out of the house?" I asked. "I assume that was what you were trying to do with all the ghosts and ghostly noise."

"I don't know what you are talking about," Elinor said. "We had nothing to do with that."

The look on her face almost convinced me that she really didn't know what I was talking about. Andrew looked as puzzled as his sister did.

It was at this point that I heard a movement behind me. At first I was disappointed, and slightly upset that Monica felt it was time for her to show herself. I had hoped that she would stay out of sight and be a witness to what was said. My thoughts were quickly forgotten when I heard her yell from off to the side.

"Nick! Look out behind you!"

As I quickly stepped to the side and began to turn around, I drew the gun from my belt. There was the loud bang of a pistol going off and I saw the bright flash of light from the mussel of a gun only a few feet away from me. I was almost sure that I heard the bullet whiz pass by me as I dove to the floor.

I returned fire immediately, not giving the assassin the chance to take a second shot at me. I could see the shadowy figure hurled backward as the 9mm slug from my pistol hit him in the upper left side of his chest. The last sound was that of a body falling to the floor, followed by a short period of silence.

It was at that moment that I heard a soft groan of someone in pain coming from behind me. I turned back around to see who it was that had been hurt.

Suddenly, the lights in the main room came on. I saw Monica standing next to the light switch for the overhead lights. The suddenness of the light caused everyone to freeze right where they were. I turned back to see who it was that had been hurt.

Next to the small table near the panel laid Elinor Mortimer. She laid slouched on the floor with her head against the wall. Andrew rushed to her side, knelt down beside her and held her, placing her head on his shoulder.

From the looks of the blood on the front of her blouse there was little hope that she would survive the gunshot wound. She opened her eyes and looked up at her brother, let out a long slow sigh and then fell limp in his arms.

I quickly turned to see who it was that had tried to shoot me in the back and hit Elinor by mistake. I stood up and walked over to the man in the dark coat lying in a heap on the floor. At first I was not sure who it was as the blast from my gun had caused him to spin around and fall face down on the floor.

I knelt down beside him and slowly rolled him over. I was surprised to see Arthur Mortimer lying in a pool of his own blood. He opened his eyes and looked up at me.

"Did I get her?" he asked in a weak, raspy voice.

"Who?" I asked.

"Elinor. Did I get her?"

I looked over to see Andrew still holding the lifeless body of his sister in his arms. He had gotten her all right, but I had gotten him. I turned back and looked down at Arthur again and nodded. There was a slight grin of satisfaction on his face as he looked up at me.

"The rest of the treasure is in the tower off the room next to mine," he whispered. "I've been hiding it from them. I took only small amounts at a time so they wouldn't notice."

So that was who had the rest of the treasure. This frail, scared old man had been taking the treasure out of the mine right under his wife's nose.

I thought back to the night when I had talked with him. Although he had appeared to be afraid of his wife, he was not so afraid of her as to prevent him from putting together a stash of his own.

"I was going to - -." He paused for a second and coughed before he continued. "To disappear. To leave her and go somewhere she could never find me."

"Did you put Elizabeth's body on the beach?"

"I had it put there." Again he coughed before going on. "I was trying to frighten Mr. Walker into leaving before he got hurt, but he wouldn't go. He called you instead," he said as his voice became weaker with each word.

"What about the ghosts?"

"I had that done, too. I even left the gold pin from the ghost's dress where Mr. Walker would find it."

So that was how Tom got the gold broach we found in his room. It had been left behind for him to make sure that he believed in the ghost.

Just then, Arthur reached up and grabbed the front of my shirt. He strained as the pain gripped him. He smiled up at me as if to tell me that he was now free. Slowly his hand let loose of my shirt and fell to the floor as he let out a long slow exhale and died. I reached down, put my hand over his face and gently closed his eyelids.

I turned and looked up at Monica standing behind me. There was nothing else we could do until the police arrived. Monica took an afghan from the sofa and covered Arthur with it. Andrew was still sitting on the floor holding his sister when I walked across the room to the phone next to the door to call the police.

CHAPTER TWENTY-ONE

I watched Andrew while we waited for the sheriff to get to the lodge. It seemed as if it took forever for a deputy sheriff to arrive at the lodge, although it was only ten or fifteen minutes. Andrew sat on the floor and held his sister the entire time. It was the first time I had seen him show any kind of affection toward anyone or anything.

By the time the sheriff's deputy arrived, everyone who had been staying at the lodge was sitting around the living room. The newlyweds were huddled in one corner of the main room holding onto each other and trying to avoid looking at the bodies lying on the floor. It was as if they were trying to avoid the reality of the situation. I could hardly blame them. After all, they were on their honeymoon.

Mr. Beresford sat quietly in a large wing-backed chair watching Mr. Thorndike grieve over his sister. He did not appear to be upset, or even one bit concerned over Andrew's loss. In fact, he didn't seem to care one way or the other.

Andrew sat on the floor still holding his sister in his arms while tears ran down his face. I found it interesting that he showed so much concern over Elinor's death and so little over the death of Miss Weatherspoon. He had not so much as lost one second of sleep over Miss Weatherspoon.

Tom had also come down shortly after the gunshots. He was now sitting in an overstuffed chair near the fireplace with his head tipped back and his eyes closed. I was sure that he was worried about what two deaths at the lodge would do to the success or failure of his business.

The first to arrive from the Sheriff's Office was Deputy Jeffrey. He looked around the room at everyone when he first came in, then began to take down names and addresses of everyone there while we waited for the ambulance and the sheriff to arrive.

When Sheriff Sam Atkins finally arrived, he walked in the front door. He stopped and stood there for a second just looking around the scene, observing where everything and everyone was located. After quickly taking in the room and the placement of the bodies, he looked at each of the guests. When he saw me, he stopped and looked at me for a second or two longer then the others as if trying to place me.

"Nick, Nick McCord, what the hell do you have to do with all of this?" he asked as he walked over toward me and stuck out his hand in greeting.

"A hell of a lot more than I had planned on, Sam," I replied as I stood up and took hold of his hand.

Sam and I go back a number of years. I had worked with him when he was a rookie on the Milwaukee Police Department. He didn't care much for the action of a big city police force so he quit. I didn't know until that moment that he moved to Sturgeon Bay and joined the Sheriff's Office and eventually was elected Sheriff.

"You want to tell me what happened here?" he asked as he looked around the room again.

"The guy lying on the floor with the afghan over him is Arthur Mortimer. He has a 9mm slug in his chest from my gun."

"You shot him?" Sam asked with a surprised look on his face.

"Yes. I thought he was trying to shoot me in the back, but he was really trying to shoot the woman over there, his wife," I said as I pointed to Elinor Mortimer.

Sam glanced over at the lifeless body of Mrs. Mortimer, and at Andrew. He then looked back at me to explain.

"Looks like he succeeded."

I took Sam aside and began to explain the whole story. While I was filling him in on what had taken place since I had arrived at the lodge, the lab men from the Sheriff's Office came in and began gathering evidence. A short while later, the ambulance came and took the bodies of Mr. and Mrs. Mortimer away.

"So what you're telling me is that I will find another body somewhere in the mine, in the icehouse or in the basement of this place, is that correct?" Sam asked as he tried to understand the bizarre goings-on at the lodge.

"That is correct," Monica added as she stood beside me holding onto my arm. "We found her in a crate in the mine, but Andrew indicated that the body may have been moved."

"You're trying to tell me that this whole thing is over treasure. Treasure that was stolen from people and ships on the Great Lakes over a hundred years ago?" he asked having a hard time believing what he had been told.

"That's right, Sam."

After hearing the complete story as best we could tell it, Sam placed Andrew Thorndike under arrest for the murder of Miss Priscilla Weatherspoon. Sam was not sure what other charges he could file at this time, but indicated that other charges would be filed as soon as everything was sorted out.

With the decision to charge Andrew with murder, and the brief questioning of the others, he released the remaining guests and allowed them to return to their rooms.

"Are there any other bodies that I might find just lying around while I'm here?" Sam asked after he watched his deputies cuff Andrew and lead him out the door.

I was not paying much attention to Sam at the moment. I was watching them lead Andrew away. I had no reason to feel sorry for Andrew, but in a way I did. He gave no resistance. He seemed to have already resigned himself to a long time in an American prison.

"Nick?"

"Oh, yeah, Sam?"

"I asked if there are any other bodies that I might find just lying around while I'm here?"

"As a matter of fact, yes," Monica said hesitantly. "There is a possibility that you will find the body of Elizabeth Samuelson's lover buried in the ice in the mineshaft."

Sam looked at Monica as if she were some kind of nut. I almost had to laugh at the expression on his face, but I thought it would be a better idea to explain.

Just as I was about to tell him what we believed, Mr. Beresford walked over to us. He had remained in the room while the others guest returned to their rooms.

"Excuse me, please, but I think I can enlighten the Sheriff on some of the history of this old house."

Sam looked at him, then at me. I sort of shrugged my shoulders and waited to hear what he could add.

"By all means, please do, Mr. Beresford," Sam said.

"I'm sorry, Mr. McCord, but I didn't tell you the complete truth earlier."

"I understand, Mr. Beresford," I replied as I waited for him to tell Sam what he knew.

"Bartholomew Samuelson did not build this house for his young and beautiful wife, Elizabeth, as most people thought. He built this house to hide the valuable items he stole from people and from ships on the Great Lakes. He was nothing more than a vicious pirate who captured ships, took what he wanted and then sank the ships with everyone on board, leaving no witnesses.

"Elizabeth was a sweet innocent girl who knew nothing about his activities as a pirate. She was young and very much in love with him, at first. As time passed, and with Bartholomew gone most of the time, she became very lonely.

"She met a young man who lived nearby. She eventually fell deeply in love with the young man and they began to have an affair. She became pregnant by the young man.

"When Bartholomew came into port and found out that she had a baby boy, he went into a rage and killed both Elizabeth and her lover by locking them in the icehouse to freeze to death. After they froze to death, he threw them into a mineshaft and covered them with water where they remained frozen until now. He left the very next day never to return, although he had planned to return to recover his treasure.

"A housekeeper found the baby in the nursery and no one around. She cared for the baby for several days, but when no one returned, she turned the baby over to the authorities. The baby, my father, was given to Elizabeth's parents and raised by them."

"What happened to Bartholomew?" Sam asked.

"It was said that he died in a storm on the lakes. Some even believed that he returned to England, which he did for a short time. But, it was discovered later that he died a poor desperate seamen in a bar fight in Brazil several years after he disappeared from here."

Sam thought about what he had been told. It was clear that there was nothing else that could be done tonight. It would be a major undertaking to remove the bodies from the mine and the mineshaft.

"I don't suppose there's any hurry in trying to find the bodies of Elizabeth's lover and Miss Weatherspoon. It's late and we are all tired. It might be a good idea if we all got some rest and proceeded with the rest of this investigation in the morning," Sam suggested.

"There is just one question that I would like answered, Mr. Beresford."

"Of course, Mr. McCord."

"What was on the piece of paper that you burned in the fireplace the other night?"

"Oh, that. It was a brief report from a private investigator that I hired to find out who you are."

I nodded that I understood.

"I will be leaving a guard on the basement to keep everyone out of there. I don't want any evidence that might be found down there disturbed until I have had a chance to examine it," Sam said.

"Mr. Beresford, I expect you will be here in the morning. I will probably have a number of questions to ask you," Sam added.

"I'll be here, Sheriff," Mr. Beresford replied.

"I'll want to talk to you, too," Sam said to me.

"We'll be here, too" I replied.

Monica and I said goodnight to Sam after Mr. Beresford had left and gone upstairs. I looked over at Tom. He was still sitting next to the fireplace with his head in his hands. He looked as if he could use a friend just about now.

"I think I should talk to Tom for a minute. I'll meet you upstairs," I said to Monica.

She glanced over at Tom and then looked up at me.

"Okay," she replied.

I stood there for a minute as I watched her as she walked away and started up the stairs. As soon as she was out of sight, I walked over to Tom and sat down in a chair in front of him.

"You okay, Tom?"

Tom looked up at me. His eyes showed how tired he was, and the lines on his face showed how depressed he had become.

"I don't know if this place will be able to make it now that there have been several murders here. Everything I have worked so hard for is going down the drain," he said softly, his voice showing how little hope he had to turn things around.

"Oh, I don't know. It seems to me that you might have to change your approach to your advertising, but I think you will be beating people away."

He looked up at me. The look on his face showed that my statement confused him.

"I don't understand?" he finally said.

"Tom, people are fascinated by the strange history of places like this. This place has one of the most colorful histories of any place in Wisconsin," I explained.

"I suppose you're right," he replied as he looked around the room.

"If you take advantage of the history of this place in your advertising, you might very well have to beat customers away."

"You're right. I could even give tours of the lodge, the icehouse and even the mine."

"Now you're thinking."

The idea of Tom still being able to make his dream of a lodge a success was giving him new hope. He still looked tired, but somehow he began to look more like I remembered him, alive and willing to take on a challenge. I was sure that it would not be long and he would be back to normal.

"I'll see you in the morning. We can talk then," I said as I watched him thinking about his future.

"Yeah, see you in the morning," he said as he stood up and began walking toward the dining room.

As soon as he was gone, I noticed that the deputy who was to keep everyone out of the basement was sitting on a chair in front of the panel. I acknowledged his presence and went upstairs to my room.

I slipped the key into the lock and opened the door. The small table lamp on the dresser was giving the room a soft glowing light. As I stepped around the corner, I saw Monica lying on my bed sound asleep. The sheet that covered her did nothing to hide the smooth lines of her body. Her soft blond hair fanned out over the pillowcase and framed the smooth texture of her fair skin.

I had to smile to myself when I noticed a damp towel hung over the back of the chair next to the bed. I thought about leaning over her and kissing her, but decided to take a shower first.

After a warm shower, I wrapped a towel around my waist and returned to my room. I turned out the light, laid my towel on the chair next to hers and crawled under the sheet next to her.

"Hi," she said as she rolled up against me, pressing her breasts against my side.

The feel of her soft, warm body made me want her. I reached over and pulled her tightly against me, wrapping her in my arms. She rested her head on my shoulder as her hand made soft light circles in the hair on my chest.

"What's going to happen to the treasure?" she asked.

"I suppose most of it will end up in a museum. Some will probably be on display here at the lodge. I doubt that it would be possible to return all the treasure to its rightful owners after all these years."

"You know that tomorrow I will have to go back to the University. My job here is finished," she said, her voice showing me how disappointed that made her.

"Yes, I know. I have to return to Milwaukee."

"I will miss you," she said in a soft hushed voice.

"I will miss you, too."

"Will you come see me, sometime?"

"I'd love to."

She lifted her head from my chest and looked at me. I could see the light from outside the window sparkle in her eyes. I rolled her over on her back and leaned down over her. Our lips met in a hard passionate kiss, a kiss that took us both away from this place if only for a short time.

A soft moan escaped from her lips as our bodies pressed together. I rose up and looked down at her face and watched a soft smile come to her lips.

"I love you," she whispered.

I slowly lowered myself over her and our lips met once again. The touch of her hands on me and the feel of her warm body under me was all it took for me to shut out the rest of the world.

Tonight we would spend making love and enjoying each other. Tomorrow we might have to go back to our jobs and our own homes, but tonight was for us. Tonight, we would escape into that private place where we could be undisturbed by the turmoil of the rest of the world.

Made in the USA
Middletown, DE
11 November 2022

14553874R00137